Linda Tegerdine, for many years, lived in a quaint village called Goldhanger near the River Blackwater in Maldon, Essex.

It was in these early years, when her family were young, that she lived in a spooky but delightful old house where indeed odd things first started to happen.

Linda has already had two children's books published, and comes from a writing family.

She hopes to achieve many more novels and already a further book is in the pipeline.

We await more of the writings of this rather unusual author extraordinaire, who now lives in Fritton on the border of Norfolk and Suffolk.

www.linda@hollycottagestories.co.uk

Round to Midnight

Linda Mary Tegerdine

ROUND TO MIDNIGHT

Vanguard Press

VANGUARD PAPERBACK

A CIP catalogue record for this title is
available from the British Library.

ISBN 978 184386 526 1

*Vanguard Press is an imprint of
Pegasus Elliot MacKenzie Publishers Ltd.*
www.pegasuspublishers.com

First Published in 2009

**Vanguard Press
Sheraton House Castle Park
Cambridge England**

Printed & Bound in Great Britain

To my Family
David, Hazel, and Andrew forever asking,
"Have you finished that book yet?"

CHAPTER 1

THE BEGINNINGS

The year opened on a distinctly pessimistic note.

The afternoon had faded quickly that misty day in the middle of January, the leaves had long past fallen off the trees, and everywhere looked bleak, cold and damp, no wind stirred anywhere at all. It was a day of huddling indoors and trying to keep warm.

I had always been a one for fanciful notions, and had always believed in the unknown since a young girl; being very much a loner I had always hoped that spirits and ghosts would visit me, but much to my deep disappointment nothing ever came, not in the earlier years anyway. I had always relied on my inner feelings, which were usually right, but now and then I seemed to have the few odd vague visions and sensations that were perhaps my imagination, or so I had thought at the time. In years to come this theory was proved wrong.

My family often laughed at me, as sometimes I had funny old-fashioned ways, but we were usually a normal happy one, even though I'm sure they did suspect me of being very slightly eccentric at times, which in all probability I was.

I wore long skirts, along with unusual tops, and scoured the shops for something different, so perhaps I looked the part.

My parents died when I was quite young, so when I married James, I had no one to help me with my two children Adam and Emma, but they were placid good children, so I did not have many problems. Their father James had always been strict with them, which I suppose helped keep them in order. They are days now far gone. Emma was single, and Adam lived only ten miles away with his partner. So with only James and I at home now, life was pretty quiet, we were both still working, but at the time little did I know that one day I would have a story to tell.

I came originally from a little village in Essex, which I had loved dearly, but one of life's misfortunes made me leave there, and move to Shropshire, where I now live. It is a very pretty village, with a wood within a few minutes' walk, which I and my dog love. Even though I am happy enough, nothing quite makes up for the life that I left behind, but that is another story, to be told perhaps another time.

On this particular Tuesday, it had been an extra busy day at work, it was also the end of the month, which means in an accounts office, loads of work to be completed, and sent, a task which I enjoyed, but found extra stressful, especially if the figures did not balance, which frequently happened, as I am not the world's best accounts manager. Then on top of that, there was shopping to be done after work, mainly because we seem to run out of everything all at once, like one does.

I cannot get organized like other people who make endless lists, then do it all at the weekend in one go.

For once on the stroke of four thirty that day I was off, supermarket first then off home, winding my way through all the rush hour traffic was a pain, and on these winter evenings it grew dark and foggy very quickly, making my journey even slower than normal, making me irritable and exhausted. I eventually arrived home. The house was in darkness, which did not worry me, as I could hear my dog barking with excitement at my arrival home.

At last, the shopping sorted, and packed away, tea done and eaten, then the dog taken for a lovely run, it was now time for me to relax.

This particular evening in January, I was at home on my own in our little terraced cottage; it was a peaceful homely house, pink on the outside with lots of little bits and pieces, that make a home a home. As you entered the front door, you saw a long hallway with a steep spiral wooden staircase. I was always frightened that my dog would fall down them in her excitement to greet me, but she never did. Beyond that you had a lounge on the left, which was filled with old pieces of pine furniture, which had a history all of its own, along with a very ancient piano dated back to the 18th Century. In the far corner beyond that, there was another lounge, where the settee chairs and television lived, along with us, if and when we had the time to sit in there; through yet another door, but still on the ground floor was the kitchen. At the end of the kitchen, was a sliding door, which entered upon a tiny passageway, which led to three doors. The one on the far left opened up onto a dining room, which overlooked the garden. This was a lovely room for having meals in and entertaining the odd guest or two. The next door led to the cellar, which was underneath the dining room; this was the only area in the house that I did not like. It had steep concrete steps going down to the cellar; it always seemed intensely cold and sinister, so I very rarely went down there. The last door was the bathroom, which also looked out upon the garden. We often kept chickens, so it was pleasant to hear them clucking as one was washing one's hair. It was an unusually long house with plenty of character as it was quite old, and I loved every inch of it, apart from the cellar.

The garden was full of pots and plants everywhere; it was a long straggly one, like the house, with a little secret garden right at the bottom of it, with a little gate. This was mine where I could read a book in peace, or just purely meditate, when one wished to be alone. The house itself was full of warmth and peacefulness, so I was never afraid to be there by myself, until the time when strange things started to happen.

After pottering about I felt weary so I decided to go to bed early. It had been a long day. I made the decision to spoil myself with a good book and a night cap, along with my beloved dog, which seemed like a good idea at the time.

It was unusual to be on my own in the house at night as my husband James was usually there with me, but for once he was away on a refresher course for a couple of weeks, which did not worry me in the slightest as I enjoyed having a little time to myself. James was a teacher, so I expect he was glad of a change of routine as well.

It was strange, but somehow right from the beginning of that evening I sensed that things were not right. The wind outside had started to pick up and howl, making eerie noises as it whirled around the house, scraping branches on the window, which sounded like somebody tapping, yet unknown to me at that time, this was the start of the strange force of things yet to come.

The book that I had taken to bed was brilliant, but somehow I could not concentrate on it, for what reason I did not know. My dog Holly who always slept on my bed seemed to be unusually nervous; her eyes kept darting towards the bedroom door, which led into the hall, beyond that the stairs. Even as she lay her head down, her eyes still kept staring towards the open door. It scared me, as she made no attempt whatsoever to shut them and was distinctly uneasy.

Cat, in fact I will call her Cat though her proper name is Hayley, had deserted me, instead of curling up beside me on the bed somewhere. She had vanished completely out of sight to sleep the night in another room maybe, which was most uncanny as she always slept quite close to me, on a chair or windowsill, which ever took her fancy, as cats do.

I remember clearly as if it were only yesterday, as the Big Ben clock downstairs chimed midnight, my eyes grew pleasantly heavy with sleep, and slowly I turned to switch the bedroom light off.

It had been turned off for several minutes, when my mind started to drift into that delicious sensation called sleep, when I felt the sudden presence of something creepy and sinister. I felt or sensed something or someone very near to me. Frantically I felt for the light switch, fumbling and knocking things over as I did so, the sudden surge of light making me blink. I looked feverishly around, but the room was empty, though to my deepening concern, my dog still had her eyes on the door, and was still visibly unsettled.

I too glanced towards it, but again nothing could be seen. What was the matter with me? I had a further strange feeling that something was lurking nearby. Just at that exact moment the stairs on the landing creaked, making me jump. I slowly drew myself out of bed as quietly as I could, then I crept stealthily towards the stairs, switching on the bright hall light as I did so.

I checked all the bedrooms, and looked underneath every bed in the house, and into every cupboard. I found Cat but nothing else. The broom suddenly fell over as I accidentally knocked it, making not only me, but my dog as well, spin hastily round. Still nothing could be seen but something was there, and watching me, I could feel it. My skin started to tingle and crawl. With my heart pounding I had another glance through everywhere, but still nothing. How very peculiar. The stairs on the landing creaked again making my heart do a double somersault. I made a smart beeline for the bed; there is a limit as to what one can take, when one is on their own. As I struggled to get between the sheets, I noticed to my dismay that my dog was still looking towards the door, as if she was guarding me from something, as though she too knew that something was there.

Keeping the light on, I drifted off into an uneasy restless sleep.

When morning came, everything was as normal, the sun was shining and at the start of another day, I pushed all the events of the night before to the back of my mind. The phone suddenly rang making me jump. "Mum are you in tonight? I have some news to tell you." My daughter Emma was always full of life and very excitable, she just adored life to the full, it was for living and she made sure she did just that.

So plans made, I took off for work. The office was again busy that day, so time went more quickly than normal. Tired out I eventually arrived home shortly after five thirty, just in time to hastily sort out a light dinner before my daughter arrived.

Promptly one hour later in Emma rushed, the events of the past evening far gone and forgotten in my mind. Time went quickly and far too fast, with my daughter deciding on a sudden holiday to India, and how long it would take her to save up for it.

Emma game me a quizzical look, "What do you think mum, if I could save one hundred pounds a month for a whole year, do you think that would get me a cheap flight to India. I just want to go back there again, it's somewhere different and so hot, perhaps you could come as well, what do you think?" I hesitated, she was certainly tempting me very well.

"Perhaps I might do, it's a long way ahead, but first you have got to start saving hard young lady if you really want to go. I must admit it would be fun to go with you, I will certainly think about it."

"Well, I am determined to go," she smiled, "it will be something to look forward to."

When we next looked at our watches it was ten thirty, hence Emma was off like the wind. "I have a good hour's journey ahead of me mum, I must be off." With a determined leap off the settee, she started to gather her bits and pieces together and within ten minutes she had gone, and all was suddenly quiet. Too quiet, the wind had started to pick up again, once more I felt nervous.

I bolted the front and back door, then the happenings of the night before jumped into my mind. How I now wished that I had spoken to Emma about it, but then she would have tossed her head the way she does and laughed. I would more than likely have joined in and felt better, for a while anyway.

How silent the house was without her, and James still away, there were a further ten nights to go on my own, before my husband returned home.

Why was it bothering me, I usually loved the freedom of the house with no one there. I had the animals; they would let me know if anyone was about, but why did I feel so despondent, it was not like me at all. I must admit I felt refreshed from the visit of my daughter and much more cheerful. We had talked and laughed a lot, but I had all the forebodings still of last night. Perhaps I was missing James. Feeling tired out physically and mentally, I concentrated on the usual nightly chores as quickly as I could, and headed for bed.

I felt a slight headache coming on, so decided not to do any reading that night; anyway I was too tired even to concentrate. Glancing at my dog I noticed that she was still uneasy and watchful as before, and that cat had disappeared once again, making my stomach churn.

I hurried up with my bath, then straight to bed. I hastily turned off the little bedroom lamp before I could start to think too much, but already I was feeling frightened. A few minutes must have passed or more when, to my horror, this horrible oppressive fear came back again. I was now once more in a terrible blind panic, and certain that something was there watching me, I could feel it. Hurriedly I fumbled for the light for the second time round, everything simply crashed to the floor including the lamp in my desperate need to put the lamp switch on.

Books, drink, pens, paper, the lot dropped onto the thick cream carpet, the water being soaked up within seconds, leaving me with an empty glass amongst other things on the floor. For what seemed ages, but probably only seconds later my eyes like a magnet went straight back to the bedroom door, which was always left open. There was something in the hall, I knew it, but it still looked empty as before. What was the matter with me? Was I imagining all of it, or was it really happening?

Feeling extremely tense yet again, I thought the best thing to do was to keep the hall light on the whole time while I was in the house by myself, or as soon as it was dark, and to keep my bedroom door tightly shut. There was a creepiness about the place which had not been there before, some presence was there but why couldn't I see it? The dog and cat sensed it so what was the problem, it looked as though it was watching and waiting, but what, I had not the vaguest idea at that point in time. It was many moons later that I had my first inkling as to what it was all about.

I followed the same pattern every night, light on, door shut, and all was well, though one night I did see a black shadow on the stairs, as though waiting for something or someone.

As usual like every other morning I'm late for work, why is it that one doodles about in the mornings, when suddenly your eyes go towards the dreaded clock, and, oh dear, time I was gone, and late again. Today was rather worse than normal; the phone rang just as one is about to turn the key in the door. Do I or don't I answer it, my head mutters to itself? I yank the offending phone off the hook, and say the usual party piece, but in very clipped peeved tones. "Are you late again my dear?" a calm teasing voice speaks on the other end of the line, who else but my husband James.

"Yes I am late, I nearly didn't answer it, is it something important you want, as I must go?" There were a few moments silence.

"Yes I am well, as you didn't ask me. But to be serious now, I cannot come home until three more days' time. Will you be alright on your own for those extra few days? I'm missing you."

"James what a time to tell me all this, you could have rung me up earlier, and yes I am alright, and yes I am missing you as well, but I must go now, I am already fifteen minutes late, hurry home." I blew him a kiss down the phone, and put the receiver down. The telephone was silent now. Why was I still so on edge? Oh well what is another three days, with that thought I made a dash for the car, dropping my handbag in my haste to get there, and wasting another few precious minutes picking everything up. The very next evening I decided to visit a friend, I was getting fed up with my own company along with a spooky house. Emma was away for a few days so I made arrangements in my lunch hour that day to see a friend of mine early that evening. I had not seen her for ages, so it would be good to see her again and catch up on all the news. I finished work promptly that afternoon, and for once was first out of the office.

Once home I made myself a quick omelette, I was trying to diet anyway, then took the dog for her run and fed her, put some fresh make-up on, then was off again into the cold night air. It turned out to be a pleasant drive and evening. It was a beautiful full moon, with the hint of frost in the air, the sort of evening which I like best.

Parking neatly, I banged on her door, looking forward to the evening. An owl was hooting in the nearby tree, what a lovely sound. The door shot open to reveal the lovely scent of apple wood burning on their wood stove, with a faint smell of casserole drifting in from the kitchen. "Have you eaten?" smiled

Maggie. "There is plenty for all of us." She caught my hand, and pulled me into the warmth of the house, and soon we caught up on the latest books out, along with all the usual chat that us folks do. When her daughter rang a few hours later on in the evening, I signalled to her that it was time I was off. I had been tempted to tell her about the cottage, but had decided not to in the end. She might have thought me a bit odd, or made her worry.

Giving her a quick peck on the cheek I was away, not giving the dark and cold outside a second thought.

Driving back home along the twisty narrow winding road took all my attention, and my thoughts were miles away. Whether it was my nervous state of mind at that time though I don't think so, but one moment the road was completely empty, then suddenly there in front of me was a vision of a monk in a hood and long flowing cloak. The monk just seemed to glide across the road; I was too astonished to be frightened. I just could not believe what I had just seen. It had been so tall, I could still see it in my mind, but it had definitely been a monk, and it had just literally drifted across the road in front of my car.

I lived within a mile of the old ruins, which many years ago, had been a highly active monastery, but that was roughly about the 12th Century. It suddenly felt at the time, as though I was beginning to have the gift of second sight as they call it. Instead of feeling excited and pleased, I was scared, what would happen next, and when.

Within ten minutes I was safely back home. I hesitated for a moment, a little anxious to go that step further indoors. I then heard my dog greeting me with her usual excited barking, I smiled, all was well. I would tell my family about the monk when I saw them all next week. In the meantime I would make discreet enquiries at work, I knew someone who might possibly be interested.

At least that took my mind off other things, and that night I slept well.

Once my husband James returned, I forgot about the scary presence. I did not even mention the sleepless scary nights to him, as I had put it all down to my vivid imagination.

I then forgot all about it, though I did mention the monk to him, he laughed, then was intrigued. That was something to be looked into further when we had more time.

Things returned to normal quite quickly. The light now went off in the hall at night, the animals slept in their usual places, and for a while everything was back to the normal routine.

Summer came, and Emma was still badgering me to go to India with her the following year. Her keenness was rubbing off onto me, so half promising that I would if James did not mind me leaving him. The warm summer weather passed far too quickly, so that the evenings started to draw in early once again, the long-range weather forecast predicted a bad winter. It looked as though we were to have a bad one with snow, that I did not mind as I love the snow, much to the disgust of people at work; they were so dull and boring. We were well into the winter months by now, when I suddenly fell ill, and developed the dreaded flu bug with a tedious chesty cough to go with it. My main concern was that I was keeping James awake at night by my high temperature and attacks of coughing, so I decided to take myself off to sleep in the study next door to our bedroom for the next few weeks, or until I was feeling better. Following that decision my nights in the study were not good, I kept waking up for no apparent reason. I then started to have terrible nightmares even though my fever had subsided, the only thing that I could put it down to, were my feelings of being ill and unsettled at that particular time.

A few nights later, I found myself waking up to the sound of myself screaming, immediately stuffing my face into the pillow so as not to wake James up in the next room. All I could remember was that in this nightmare someone was always chasing me until I was cornered, then I always woke up screaming, but I would never ever see its face, all I knew was that it had the shape of a human body and a cloak.

Some nights after my screaming fits, I would hear the wind or branches tapping on the glass windows outside, and the wind blowing. The dreams always terrified me, so that would be the time that I would always creep back into the safety of the other bedroom, and snuggle up to James for comfort, until my coughing fits started up again, when I would silently return to the study and a lonely bed.

He too was often woken up by my screams, but he kept his thoughts to himself.

The house itself was old. It had heavy old-fashioned white sash windows, that perhaps loosened in the wind to make the tapping noises, or that was my thought at first.

As you went through to the kitchen downstairs, there stood a door to your left, which led you to the cellars beneath. I rarely went down there, that was the only part of the house that I really hated, it spooked me out. My study, where I was sleeping at that time, was just above it. Not until much later on did we discover a vital clue about that cellar, and why it was always so deathly cold.

Weeks went by, I looked and felt fully recovered and back to full power, but still the bad dreams came, why I just could not fathom out. At this time I was doing a lot of work in the study in the evenings, so I was in that room quite frequently. Another strange thing was that I had started to sleep again in my old bedroom with James, as he did not like me sleeping in the study. I would settle down and drift off quite easily, then every night I started to wake up in the region of two in the morning. Once awake I was unable to get back to sleep again. If I slipped back into the bed in the study, I would get to sleep straight away, as soon as my head touched the pillow. But then to my deepening concern, stranger things were now starting to happen.

A horrible smell of decaying would fill the room like a mist; it seemed to keep gently drifting in and out of the study like a breeze. It gradually filled the whole room. The animals became restless again. They would go out, only to come back in half an hour later, then go out again. They acted as though they were continually on edge, but why?

I mentioned it to James, who could not think what it was, and did not seem unduly concerned. My first thoughts about the weird smell, was that the cat must have bought something into the room, and hidden it under the bed or something silly, though on reflection it always rose up just where my desk was, or by the window overlooking the courtyard below, where beneath that was the cellar. One evening I decided to move every box and piece of furniture there, just in case the cat had come in with a mouse or bird. A thorough search proved negative, nothing to be found. My next thoughts were put down to drainpipe problems, but on further investigations nothing was to be revealed, even James could not puzzle it out. Why, he reasoned did the smell only appear in one room? Surely if it were environmental it would be in all of the rooms or the upstairs ones at least, where the study was.

James scratched his head in bewilderment. "The thing is, Catherine, what I find most odd, is that have you noticed that I never smell anything when I go in there by myself. Another thing to ponder is that if the cat had caught something, the smell of it would be there the whole time surely, I just simply cannot understand it at all."

"Well, I just cannot make it out either, but it is getting revolting, even the animals go out, there must be something there." With that parting shot, I went into the kitchen to prepare dinner.

James followed me through to the kitchen, sensing that I was disturbed and worried. "We should be having a card from Adam shortly. I wonder how he is liking Scotland. Perhaps we ought to go away next year, we don't seem to have had a holiday for ages." He kissed the top of my head as he went back thankfully to his Sunday paper, and his favourite armchair.

Several more weeks must have gone by when something even more sinister was discovered: this strange awful smell only happened after dark, and this knowledge was beginning to concern me. During the day, the room was calm, fresh smelling and peaceful. Then upon entering the room in the evenings it was the same, but as soon as I was seated at my desk, within five minutes the smell would creep up by the side of me.

It was the most terrible smell of something decomposing. It started with a slight scent, then little by little grew stronger. By far the most frightening thing of all, was when I realised that the spirit or whatever it was only came when I was alone in the room. It was a sinister smell that filled the whole room. It felt really like a mist rising and creeping across the room, sometimes starting from my desk, then at other times from the window and courtyard below.

One day I yelled for James to come up and smell it for himself. Upon entering the room, his whole body swung back in shock; his look was of sheer horror and disbelief. His face went pasty white, then he whispered, "It's horrendous whatever is it." He looked down at his arms. "Look I have gone all goose pimply and I feel sick," then quickly went from the room.

It eventually dawned on us, both at the same time, that did this awful sinister thing or smell belong to what we thought was the spirit world, might after all be environmental, so we decided to experiment first. James would go and sit in the study for several evenings on his own to see whether it would come with just him being there. I kept well out of the way, only calling him to come back downstairs when the clock struck ten in the evening.

Night after night James sat up there for two solid weeks running. I still kept well out of the way and did not enter the room once – James religiously taking up newspapers and books to read, to fight his boredom at being up there. When the two weeks were up, my husband put up his hands in disappointment and said, "I give up, nothing will come while I'm up here, you have a go." He gave up at nine thirty that night, and went thankfully downstairs to make a cup of tea, believing that everything was over, but he was badly mistaken.

Once he had disappeared down the stairs, I sat myself down in the study with a letter to write, but it was a different story then. It seemed only one minute before I sensed it was going to come, it was actually telling me, the words were coming through my head, then within a few seconds it was there getting stronger and stronger. I banged my letter down, slammed the door, and rushed downstairs to James. "It hasn't gone at all," I said to him, "it's just been waiting for me to come, and for you to go." I was pale now and getting tearful. What could we do, what was it? I must already have said that sentence at least fifty times already.

It was as though the spirit was waiting for me, and me alone, but why, oh why, did it not go? This thing was beginning to haunt me, it was as though it was starting to possess me. What a frightening thought, and how could I end it?

James had given up now going into the study, but for me it got worse. Whenever I now went into that room, the scent or mist, whatever it was seemed always to be lurking and waiting for me. It would appear within a few minutes, and I would always know, as it would enter my thoughts first.

Nerves on both sides were getting tetchy and stretched. Even the animals were hesitant upon entering that room, and Cat just never went in there now. We got as far as talking of moving, as I was having visions of dead bodies underneath the floorboards and decaying – the things that your mind thinks of when under stress is unbelievable.

This latest idea of mine, of perhaps a corpse underneath the floorboards started to pray on my mind, so hence late one evening, the force came yet again, as I sat at my desk. It was late; I was tired, and had taken enough of the evil creature or force.

I felt beads of perspiration on my forehead, and felt myself going pale, suddenly I got myself worked up into a frantic fury, and started pulling the carpet up, then heaving and ripping floorboards up, moving furniture and beds as I went. I ripped everything apart. The room was in utter chaos. I just wanted every inch searched underneath the floorboards. With my heart pounding, in case I found something, I sniffed, felt, touched, and looked, really believing that I would find a corpse or decomposed body. What a horrible thought, or worse still a rotting hand, or foot, it did not bear thinking about, and made me search even more like a maniac. I felt like a bloodhound, searching and searching, but finding nothing. This was too much, I just could not take it any more, so ended up sitting on the edge of the bed, and just cried and cried. It seemed to be never ending. I felt and looked utterly exhausted. A warm wet nose nudged onto my hand; I gently stroked my dear dog's head, knowing that she was doing her best to comfort me.

James had heard me pulling the floorboards and carpeting up, but had very wisely left me to it, knowing full well that I wouldn't find anything. He was positive it was something from the spirit world, but I had yet to be convinced. Leaving the room in utter chaos, I went slowly down the stairs, and sat beside my husband, tears of frustration and anger pouring down my face as I did so.

His eyes turned towards mine and quietly he said, "You found nothing?" Numbly I shook my head, and started to sob again. He held me close until my crying subsided, then said to me gently, "I will come up to the study with you, and double check everywhere, then we can decide together what we are going to do."

He looked distant as though he felt troubled. I realised that he was as worried as I was; there was no joking or banter from him today, and he did not hold my hand. We were up against a big problem, which we did not know how to solve.

James did exactly the same as I did: checked and smelt under floorboards, and looked in every nook and cranny that he could find. He then shook his head and stood up. "There is simply nothing there Catherine. I don't think it will solve anything, but I will ring the Environmental Department in the morning, to ask them to come out to see what they can make of it. Perhaps it's some gasses leaking somewhere, or a sewage problem. I just don't know, but perhaps they might have an answer, if not back to the drawing board, that is the best that I can suggest at present. We had better start to clear all this mess up in here, and put the floorboards back and forget about it for the night. Now come on, let's be off to bed, shut the study door for goodness sake, and forget all about it for the night." With that he gave me a hug and held me very tightly, then said, "Be off, bed woman, now." He felt so solid, so safe. Was it me going deranged and imaging things, or was it really happening?

I did not need asking twice. I was really down and tired, but tomorrow was a day that had not even been touched yet, so who knows we might have the answer soon.

I slept well that night, no nightmares, no waking up at two and four in the morning; I must have been utterly exhausted. In the morning James kept his promise and rang the Health Department, and explained what the problem was. They told him that they would come out to visit us within the next week, and would let us know by post when they would be coming out.

In actual fact, it took them three weeks in all, three weeks of anxious waiting. They came out twice to the cottage at different times, the second time they left a note to say nothing could be found, but they would be sending us a letter. During all this time, I had kept completely out of the study, but I needed to get back to my work, which was getting behind, but until I had received an official letter from them, something was holding me back from going in there.

I also dreaded the nightmares. If I went back to sleep in there, they would surely return. I still kept on waking up at two and three in the morning, but I kept with James for safety, but I felt myself getting exceedingly tired.

The letter eventually arrived after weeks of waiting. It came before I went to work that day, but I did not have the courage to open it until James returned that evening. It was as we both thought, negative. The letter that they sent to us was as follows:

Re: Odour Complaint.

I refer to your recent complaint received by this Department regarding the above, and subsequent visit by myself. At the time of this visit the odour was not evident. The inspection did not reveal any obvious likely cause of the decomposing type of odour you described.

We have in the past received complaints from various different people complaining of odours which you have described, but unfortunately due to the nature and occurrence of this odour, the Department is unable to offer any further assistance with this matter, though you might find it of some help, to contact your Church, who might be able to throw some light on this matter.

Yours sincerely,

R. Jimbob.

We had known deep down, that it was not any human problem, and that it must belong to the spirit world.

Upon receiving the letter, we were both very quiet. We had really known in our bones, that it was something in ghost form, but how to deal with it was the vital next question.

By now things were worsening again. Even at work and out driving in my car, I had sudden scents of it, so it was getting closer and closer to me. Something had to be done very soon, before it completely entered my head and turned me insane.

The back door suddenly crashed open making both our hearts lurch. We both spun round to see the tall good-natured face of our son pop his head in through the door. "It's only me folks, my you looked shocked, did I startle you both. I'm so sorry I did not mean to make you jump. I only have ten minutes, as I'm on my way to see a clairvoyant, but I don't seem to have given myself enough time to get there hence the rush. It's my first visit, so I don't really want to be late."

James and I looked immediately at each other. We both had the same thought in our minds. Why had we not thought of a clairvoyant before, surely she would be able to throw some light on our problem. James spoke first. "What is the clairvoyant's name?"

"I believe she is called Amidyne, but I don't remember her surname. Someone at work said that she was pretty good, and I feel as though I am in need of a bit of guidance at the moment. Why are you thinking of going dad? I didn't think you approved of that sort of thing, in fact a bit old-fashioned about it, or so I thought."

"Have you got Amidyne's number on you?" said James quickly. "I wouldn't mind going to see her myself one of these days."

"Sure dad I'll write it down now, before I forget, then I will let you know what she says about me; it must be ages since I last saw one."

"I hope she is good, they are not cheap nowadays," muttered James.

Glancing at his watch, "Goodness five more minutes, then I must be off, as I am not sure of the way." Adam had his coffee, refused any food, kissed the cat, then was gone, typical of him, and so like his sister, always in a rush and flying about.

There was silence for a few minutes, both of us deep in thought, wondering who would be the first to speak.

"Ring the clairvoyant now, just in case she is booked up for months ahead."

"But what shall I say to her?" taking James's empty cup as I did so.

"Just tell her the whole story from the beginning to the end." With that he walked out of the door his face grim.

Action was evidently being called upon on my part, so gritting my teeth, I took up Adam's piece of paper and then walked to the phone and rang her number. Surprisingly she answered straight away. I felt so stupid trying to describe everything to her that had happened, and squirmed at the prospect; it all seemed to be so far fetched. Would she believe me, or think I was someone who had lost their mind?

Amidyne listened to me very carefully, then when I had finished, she sounded very sympathetic, and seemed to believe me. She told me she had heard of these cases before, but sometimes they could be difficult to handle, then said that I would have to wait a couple of months before I could see her, as she was so booked up, but in the meantime advised me definitely not to sleep at all in that room, and to go in there as little as possible until she could come, to help us further. She would pray for some spirits to come and try and guide it on its way. Amidyne seemed to think it was a lost force or spirit, belonging to the next plane, which had attached itself only to me. Like the spirit that was haunting me, I also had in my past a very sad life with deep pain, which had perhaps drawn the spirit to me, or so the clairvoyant seemed to think. She tried to reassure me as best as possible, and said she had come across this sort of problem before. It sometimes took a while, but it could be done. "I really would come out sooner if I was able to manage it, but my mother is ill, so I just cannot spare the time. If things get really desperate, ring me again, and I will do an emergency visit. If I don't hear from you, I'll arrive on the day which we have arranged, take care, goodbye." With that the phone was put down gently but firmly.

James meanwhile had come downstairs to listen to the conversation. He pulled a face. "We have no option, we will just have to be patient and wait my dear."

CHAPTER 2

WALK IN THE FOREST

The final straw came, when late one Sunday afternoon, I decided to take my dog for a walk in the nearby woods before it got too dark. It was already getting dusk, so I hurried myself up. I always loved walking through the woods on my own with my dog, whether it was daylight, dusk or dark, smelling the freshness of the pine and heather. I never seemed to be afraid. Not like my daughter, who would be petrified when she arrived at the first tree, or heard a startled deer dive into the bushes, and she jumped at the slightest noise. She always said I ought to be a rabbit, as I knew the woods inside out, and seemed never ever to get lost, or not know where I was, no matter how far I went.

On this particular afternoon in late autumn, the dark comes upon you quickly and suddenly, one moment it is light, then a very dim dusk. I had gone further and deeper into the woods than I had intended. I call them woods, but really I suppose it is a bit like a forest as it is so large. The darkness suddenly started to fall quickly, so I decided to turn back and head for home. I remember that I was deep down in the old dense part of the wood, where the undergrowth was extremely dense. I had been following a faint deer track through the bracken, when I saw a drift of mist across my path, when everything as if by magic, was suddenly dangerously quiet, and very still – a deep hush seemed to have fallen upon the woods, so deathly quiet and abnormally still.

Glancing down I saw some very old and ancient paving slabs, though on second thoughts, they looked like head stones of some sort, perhaps an old burial ground which I had never ever seen before, even though I had been down that part of the wood often. I stood looking for a few minutes feeling the wind, cold now on the back of my neck and shivered. There were goose pimples on my arms, and for some unknown reason I felt sick. It was better to keep moving, walking now in the almost darkness amongst the trees it needed all my concentration, I just could not think, I dare not think. I wrapped my arms around myself, but for no reason I had never felt so afraid or so alone in my life before.

At that point, my eyes seemed to start blurring, and a misty haze seemed to appear again from nowhere. My dog that always stays close to me started to growl. I bent to stroke her and then saw that the ridges on her back were standing up like needles. She kept very close to me, as though she too was scared and then she started to give a deep throaty menacing growl. All of a sudden without hesitation, tail between her legs she was off. She swiftly started to run like a thing possessed. Whatever is wrong? She never ever runs off and leaves me and within seconds she seems to have completely disappeared. Where had my dog gone, and why? What had happened to her? Please let her be safe, rather the spirit have me, than my much loved dog.

It is now my turn to start running, a feeling of panic is upon me also, as I know that whoever is haunting me is right there waiting in the shadows for me, and for some reason I am in the most terrible danger. I feel something very near to my throat. My hair then seems to stand up on end, even my arms are bristling. The air is very cold and it feels like tiny cobwebs on my face.

I'm running now in a blind panic, I run and run. I must get away; my dog has completely deserted me. I feel something now touch my head, like an invisible hand, so close I can almost smell it, and feel it. I'm crashing through bushes, unknown paths; I seemed to have lost all sense of direction. The wood which I knew so well, now seems sinister and unwelcome. I staggered blindly on, running as I have never run before. I am so out of breath now, but somehow I still keep running for dear life. Something then touches my cheek. Whatever it is seems to be playing games with me. I know it's there, but it's letting me keep running, but for how long, I just don't know. All I know is, that it is still there. I go faster, getting more and more panicky and hysterical, with deep choking noises coming from within my throat. Is it really me making that awful noise? I now know for certain deep down that whatever is after me, is from the spirit world, and that same thing wants me to join it. I can sense this spirit putting these thoughts into my head. It is now so very close, but I just cannot seem to outrun it.

Panic is now taken over by sheer terror, run, run, run, is all I can think of, it is pulling at me again trying to take me over, as my body gradually starts to feel lighter as though going into a cloud onto the next plane. I give another short burst of running, but know at any moment my end is near, when suddenly, I burst out on the farm track which leads up to the main road near my cottage. I turn around knowing full well that I have only just beaten the force, that I am safe for the moment. I can feel it is still lurking on the edge of the wood, willing me to come back in. Somehow I know that on the road it will not dare to venture – too many other earthly souls about to see and hear. How I managed to escape into the lane before it was to late, I just don't know. My legs now seem like heavy bricks, but eager to get back home just in case it attacks me again. I break into a steady trot; my eyes are straining into the distance, just in case it appears again in front of me. My eyes then see something standing very still near the next bend in the road. I feel weak with the thought of this, as I know I cannot take any more. I am really now at breaking point. The spirit I feel is still watching me. I can see it standing very still and silent in the shadows. Do I turn back or keep going? My instinct tells me to keep going, to turn back now, I would almost be certain to be taken away by the spirit. The small shadow in the distance suddenly starts to come towards me, my heart racing I see then that it is now running towards me. I hear a faint bark, then more excited barking. Never before or again have I felt so relieved; it is my dog, Holly. Somehow she had escaped out of the wood and just waited for me to return, so faithful and loyal, right to the end.

She is barking and barking with joy and excitement, relief at finding me, and myself crying with delight and hugging her at the same time. I am just so relieved to have found her safe and sound, I look behind me, and see the shadow still lurking amongst the trees so know the spirit is still waiting in there for me. Will it then wait for me in the study? I just could not wait to get home to James, and tell him all that had happened. He would be horrified like I was.

Up the little lane I ran and half walked, still very uneasy and scared, but I knew, as my dog was now with me again, that the force was keeping hidden, for a while anyway. It was still near, moving up with me as I went as fast as I could along the path, but for some reason, it would not venture from the wood. I still moved quickly, but trying to think at the same time, never again would I turn out at dusk or when it was dark into the wood. I had narrowly missed death by seconds and sheer luck. I could just about see the end of the lane. Getting panicky once again, I quickened my speed until I was off the lane and onto the road. I saw our cottage was now within sight, only a few more houses and I would be home.

I again felt sick and weak, nearly passing out with exhaustion and mainly fear.

Bursting through the front door, I yelled hysterically for James, who came running to the door immediately. "Whatever has happened?" With a look of deep concern on his face, he dragged and half carried me to the nearest chair. Feeling utterly drained by now and still terrified, I told him step by step everything that had taken place in the woods that evening, so much so, that by the time I had finished he was now as white as I. The only thing that now looked completely at ease was the dog, flat out fast asleep, with not a care in the world.

My world was in shatters, what was I going to do?

James was the first one who spoke. "Amidyne, the clairvoyant, will not be coming for another two months. In the meantime, we must keep the study door shut, and on no account will you go in there. If you need any paper work or books, tell me, and I will go in and get it for you. Is that understood? Under no circumstances whatever, do you go into that room, I absolutely forbid it, do you hear?"

I just could not speak. I nodded a tearful yes to him, but failed miserably to answer. I still could not believe all that had happened. Why did the spirit want me so badly, and what would happen to me when it did so? I started to tremble, reaction was setting in, and I started to shake all over. Once I started I just could not seem to stop myself; my teeth started to chatter. I tried to speak, but it all came out mumbo jumbo. James hugged and hugged me, until at last I started to quieten down, then the sobs started. Once they began I did not seem to stop for ages, even the poor dog woke up to give me a wet lick or two, and to lay beside me.

Sitting there utterly drained and tired, I felt James get up.

"We are both in need of a drink, have we any sloe gin left?" I was still too weak to answer, but heard him fumbling about in the wine rack, then go to the cupboard, presumably for some glasses.

The sloe gin found, he gave me the fullest glass I had ever drank before. "If this keeps up, I will need to make some more," I feebly whispered.

A good five minutes must have gone by, when I felt James's hand creep in mine.

"I think in view of what has happened this evening, we must be prepared to put the house up for sale. It looks as though this force or spirit seems determined to either make trouble, or to take your life. Either way we cannot risk it, whatever its intention is. I'm so sorry I know how you love it here, but we just cannot take that chance."

I nodded stupidly, unable to speak, as I knew that I did not want to move away from this cottage, but knew perhaps that was

39

the only answer, or was it? We were both silent for a few moments, both thinking our different thoughts and what to do next. With an unexpected burst of anger I touched James's hand.

"But what if the spirit follows us to the next house that we move to; we have to make certain that it cannot do so." With that outburst, I went quiet again; all the thinking must be left to James tonight. I felt as though I would never ever be the same again. I just hated this thing that was after me. It was destroying my life, or perhaps ours. Perhaps it was jealous of James, perhaps it was trying to put a strain on both of us, so that we would split up, then the spirit would have me all to itself, but why, so many whys?

The thought now that was in both of our minds – could this thing follow us to another part of the country, or would it just give up for good, and return to its own plane. What was the history of this house; there must be a connection somewhere. Had someone died here? My mind was buzzing; we were both as nervous as each other, thinking the same thoughts.

James had been silent since my short outcry, when the telephone rang shrilly in the hall. We both nearly jumped out of our skins, but causing us to laugh together as we did so. At least it lessoned our tension slightly.

"If it's for me, tell them I have gone to bed with a headache, I just don't want to speak to anyone tonight no one at all."

James did as he was told, and ambled slowly off to the phone. He was gone what seemed to be a long time, or perhaps I had dropped off to sleep for a little while, the sloe gin was good and I did not really care anymore. Every bone in my body seemed to be spent out. I needed a good hot bath and bed, with as James said, the study door shut firmly always from now on.

Eventually James returned from the hall, "That was Emma, she says she is going to come over tomorrow. She wants you to go shopping with her into town, to help her choose a dress for some party or other. I was only listening to half what she was saying, sorry. I just hope I said yes and no in the right places. She hopes you will be better by the morning, and hopes it isn't the flu, as it is not like you to have a headache, but anyway she will ring again before she comes in the morning."

I patted the settee. "Come and sit down," I spoke softly. "I have just had a tiny thought. Supposing as a trial, I book a holiday by myself in Cornwall just for a week, with the dog. She will keep me safe, then I will know for sure whether it will follow me, what do you think of that idea?" My own heart was already sinking at the thought of it.

"I don't like the idea at all of you going on your own, but on the other hand we won't know until you do so, but whatever you do I am still going to put the house on the market while you are finding out, then if it does follow you, we will be prepared. Are you going to go Cornwall before Amidyne comes or not?" He withdrew his hand, as though the evening's events were just too much for him, so much to think of, and what to do for the best was his most important thought, besides being as scared as I was.

"What will you do, if it turns up late one night while you are in Cornwall? You will be terrified all on your own. What if it comes to you there, what will you do? I just don't like it, definitely not on your own, it could do anything. I really do not think you ought to go?"

41

Whilst James had been talking, I had still been thinking,

"I don't want to go on my own at all, but can't you see, that this is the only way we can find out whether or not it will follow me if we move. I must go. If it does come to me there, I will just walk out. Whatever time of day or night, I will jump in the car and head straight for home." I could tell that James was not happy about the situation at all, but what else could we do?

"But what will happen if the force comes while you are asleep," James spoke quietly, but full of concern. "You will not know it's there until it is too late."

Speaking more cheerfully than I felt, "I will leave a lamp on all night, that usually does the trick, as spirits are supposed to prefer the darkness. I will know if it's there, as the mist and smell will come first, but anyhow I have had more than enough for one night, let's be off to bed and discuss it tomorrow in the daylight. It will be best if we sleep on it."

With that finishing remark, James stood up. "I suppose you're right as always, but I am still going ahead with a visit to the estate agents in the morning, just in case we have to sell up, so don't try to persuade me otherwise, as I will not listen. While you finish off downstairs, I will go up and make sure the study door is shut, then I'll run a lovely hot bath for you, how's that for service." He laughed, then away he went up the stairs.

How I wished that I could laugh as well, but deep down within my body I felt as though we were just at the beginning of this nightmare. How was I going to cope? All I could do was to hope and pray that things would return to normal very soon, which I somehow doubted.

When we both awoke the next morning, we realised thankfully that it was Saturday. I felt worn out, and James seemed edgy and quiet, a sure sign that he was extremely worried.

I then remembered to my dismay that I was supposed to be going shopping with Emma today, perhaps it would do me good to take my mind off other things. We always had fun together Emma and I, especially if we were spending money.

At that moment the phone rang downstairs. Turning to James I said, "That will be our Emma, I'll take it." I then quickly bolted down the stairs, colliding with the dog as I did so, suddenly realising that she had not been out yet, and would be wanting her breakfast and walk. Why did we always seem to be rushing about so? Whatever day of the week we were always dashing about.

It was Emma. Yes I would meet her in the car park near the market at eleven this morning, and no I would try not to be late, though I bet I was – be late for my own funeral that's me.

Phone put down, I give the dog her food, feed the cat, do my face, change into my doggie walking gear, then grab her lead and away. I go towards the wood, but stay well away from where I, and my dog, ventured last night. Even she seemed to be a little hesitant upon entering them, as though she remembered the happenings of last night as well. Once in the wood I still felt slightly nervous, and kept glancing around me, but I must admit I did not feel anything there at all that morning, much to my relief. I felt sure that if I kept to my walks even if I entered deeper into the woods, if I made them in daylight, it would be okay. It was the night-time I must be very careful of, and never ever venture in them alone at that time. That decision made, I felt slightly better. The sun was shining, the birds were singing, and I was going to see my daughter today, what would be, would be. I felt strong enough at that moment to cope with anything. Glancing at my watch, I hastened my speed, nine thirty already, not much time left by the time I got home, then on to meet Emma. It would take me thirty minutes for the drive alone, oh well it would take my mind off other things hopefully.

So much traffic, the road always seemed to be busy into town nowadays; as usual I was at least ten minutes late when I saw Emma. We gave each other a hug, then hurried into the town. The day was so much fun. We shopped till we dropped, as the saying goes, both penniless as usual, and with aching tired feet, we call it a day. We had both spent and bought clothes that we did not really need. We both had a good chat, with plenty of hysterical laughter, along with a beautiful lunch, my only wish at that time, was that my daughter lived nearer to us. That would really be perfect, for the time being that could not be so, perhaps one day.

Time now to say our goodbyes. "You look a bit peaky mum, do be careful won't you. Have you still got your headache? Don't forget to let me know when you are going to have this holiday of yours in Cornwall. You are brave to be going on your own. I can't think why dad is not going with you, it won't be the same on your own." She spoke in a hurry, anxious now to get home and beat the rush.

"I just need a break on my own, that's all. It will be good for me to get away from everything, and just do my own thing, I have been working very hard lately. I will talk to you sometime in the week, it's been a lovely day, see you soon." With that we kissed each other goodbye, then went our separate ways.

I always feel a bit sad when I leave her, I suppose most mothers feel like that, but with other things to think about, the feeling soon goes, much to my relief. Keeping my eye on the traffic, I put my foot down and head for home. As I turn into our driveway, I had an urge to look up at the study window, half expecting to see a shadow there, but nothing is there, not even in my imagination.

As I enter the kitchen on the table I see a couple of blue estate agents' cards, so guess that James has kept his promise of last night, but I decide to say nothing and to ignore them, hoping it will pass without action.

The weekend passed peacefully enough, even the next few weeks after that, perhaps lulling us into a false sense of security, but more things were set to happen.

Still keeping the study closed at all times, James had reason to get out of bed one night, only to discover the bathroom light on, and the study door open. When suddenly he heard the television go on downstairs, at that precise moment in time, James told me afterwards that I started screaming and screaming. He rushed in the bedroom to find me utterly hysterical and had to force me awake. When I had gathered my mind together and listened to what James was telling me, we both got up to investigate the television downstairs. It was on, but neither of us had left it so. Also who had turned the bathroom light on, and left the study door open, when we both knew it had been shut? We were both tired and irritable at being woken up in the middle of the night; surely the force was not going to start opening doors, and switching things on. We had heard tales of things doing so, but never in a million years did we think it would happen to us.

"Good thing I went to the estate agent yesterday, if this is the sort of thing that is going to happen next," said James, then with a grunt he went back to bed, leaving me awake for the rest of the night worrying.

I rose early the next morning, unable to have a lie in like James. I decided to take a shower, hoping to make the events of the previous night disappear. As I soaped myself down, I noticed that my shoulder seemed to be very sore and tender, so on hearing James making a move, I tossed the towel around me, and sauntered back into our bedroom.

"James be a dear and have a look on my shoulder, have I been bitten by a gnat or something, it's very tender?"

He turned slowly round, like he does, to have a close look, but he did not say anything, everything was quiet. "James what's the matter, can you not see anything, it does hurt?"

James was still very silent, until at last he spoke.

"Yes I see something, there are a load of deep fresh scratches on your back, I just don't believe it, this is ghastly, this must have happened when you were having your nightmare last night, it's just unbelievable. We just cannot keep going on like this."

If James was horrified, I was petrified. This was happening to me, it was my body, what else was this spirit doing to me, without my knowledge? I could not remember what had happened in my nightmare, only that I was being chased by someone, and cornered somewhere in a derelict house, that was all I could ever remember, but I had had those nightmares before, but never with the scratches, what else could this spirit do?

This thing was really mentally, and now physically, taking over my life. I just wanted to get out of the house and run, and run, well away from this little cottage that I had grown to love so dearly, until now.

I knew that my nightmares were increasing, but now scratches. I must get away to Cornwall as soon as possible, perhaps the break away would disturb its pattern, perhaps it might disappear in my absence. I doubted it very much, but it was worth a try, before I had a nervous breakdown.

I could not have time off from my office, for another seven weeks, so my holiday would have to be put off for a little while. I had already been looking through some brochures for a little cottage in Cornwall, and had found the ideal one. It was situated near the cliffs in North Cornwall, but only a short distance from where my brother lived, so if I had any problems or visits from my friend the spirit, I would not be far from him. The thought of all this cheered me up immensely, as Cornwall was my second home, as I had been there so often.

Meanwhile the cottage at home was not up for sale as yet, but James only had to ring the agents and it would be full steam ahead. His reasoning was to get everything in order, just in case things got really bad. That way if necessary we could be out of Broome Cottage within the month.

The charming study would then return to a dull bedroom, and life will be better if ever I find a pleasanter place to work or idle in, apart from the spirit force which was now there.

Today was Sunday, so I attempted to weed out the right hand cum junk cupboard behind the bookcase and to empty the drawers in the small desk, while James, for a change, was preparing the dinner.

It was a tedious and melancholy business sorting through old letters, photographs, drawings and so on. One keeps on coming across a person or scene long forgotten, and just as the souvenir falls into the wastepaper basket, one realises that it was the only link with that particular piece of the past, which otherwise would have been forgotten forever. Can one therefore afford to throw it away?

So the lesson seems to be, stick your photographs and paraphernalia, in a book and record your acquaintances by keeping a diary.

All this simply means is that I hate moving and pulling up my roots, even the thought of it makes me irritable and anxious. Books lose all their personality away from their familiar shelf, restored to their original dirty jackets; they resemble a person standing in a cosy room with their overcoat on, which destroys peace of mind.

I make myself get rid of the small bundles of letters, which is all past history, with slight misgivings.

More of this gloomy business of turning out the past and uprooting the present is to come I fear, if we do decide to definitely move.

By the time I had cleared a few drawers and cupboards out, whilst reminiscing over my past life, I heard James calling me down for dinner. Goodness that time already, I must have been upstairs for three hours or more, how engrossed I must have been!

The weather forecast today, had been a warning of snow and ice; the bitterly cold wind was already seeping through the sashes of our old window frames. Perhaps after dinner I would put a huge log on the fire, then sitting with James in our favourite armchairs, we could discuss what next to do about the evil presence which now haunted this house.

Would it keep returning, or should we move from the cottage, before it changed us, and our lives?

A sad little mood of morbidity then overtook me.

Whatever was the matter with me today? Perhaps after lunch we ought to go out to visit our Adam. We had not seen him since his visit to the clairvoyant; that surely would help to cheer me up.

A voice called up the stairs, making me drop my sheaf of papers with a start, so deep in thoughts had I been.

The voice was clear and positive.

"Dinner is on the table my dear, will you come down or would you like it on a tray up in the study?"

My head cleared instantly. "What a stupid question is that?" I shouted back with a laugh. "Of course I will come down, give me two minutes to tidy up and I will be with you." Hastily clearing things away, I was down the stairs as quickly as I could. I suddenly realised that I was hungry. What a treat to have Sunday dinner cooked for me. James was a brilliant cook, better perhaps than I.

There before me, piled high on the largest plate that he could find, was beef, Yorkshire pudding, roast potatoes, along with a lovely selection of vegetables. Perhaps I would feel more cheerful after my meal. A cork popped, wine as well, red my favourite, my I was being spoilt today.

I knew I looked a bit peaky; perhaps a walk after dinner instead of visiting Adam would be a better idea, especially if snow was on the way.

"Catherine you're not listening to me." James was looking at me with growing concern. "Are you alright, you look miles away?"

With a grin I nodded. "I was just wondering how I was going to attack this delicious looking dinner, you really have done well, thank you." I sat down and concentrated on my meal. I would put everything out of my mind until after our walk, time enough then to sit by the log fire, and to wonder what to do next.

CHAPTER 3

SNOWED IN

It was getting on well into the afternoon, by the time we had eaten and finally cleared away. We put our coats on rather reluctantly, looking briefly at the sky as we did so. It looked heavy with snow, but as owners of a dog who was used to her afternoon walk, we had no choice in the matter but to go out.

The blast of cold wind hit us as soon as we opened the front door, tiny specks of snow already starting to fall and it was getting dark very quickly. Dragging on our scarves we hurried down the front path.

Once into the forest it really started to snow heavily. The pine trees looked so lovely in the falling snow; the flakes became larger and larger making our dog rush about like mad in wild excitement. I love the snow; it always seems to bring back happy memories of childhood days, when there were no worries or cares. What a long time ago now it all seemed, what days of bliss they were, though I did not realise it at the time.

A hand touched my elbow. "Come on Catherine I think it is time to turn back, the snow is really starting to fall heavily now.

I don't fancy being caught in the forest in this weather, especially with our spirit lurking about." James called to Holly our Labrador, then slowly we turned for home. Thankfully we plodded back, both of us deep in our own thoughts, knowing that when we returned to the cottage, we must sit down and decide what to do. I felt deep down that we should not move at the moment, but it was persuading James to stay which would be the problem. He knew as well as I, that the spirit was only after me, and that frightened him.

We arrived back home just in time; the snow had turned into a raging blizzard. As we pushed the gate open, we could only just make out our cottage amidst a swirling mass of snow, the ice and snow already beginning to freeze hard and feel crunchy beneath our feet.

Within the hour, there was at least an inch of snow on the front doorstep. Hurriedly, I turned the key in the lock. A sudden blast of warm air hit us, making us realise how cold it was outside, but somehow it seemed unnaturally quiet and eerie indoors. I glanced at the calendar on the wall, it did not seem possible that we were already well into March. How quickly the year was going, possibly I could plan for a week to Cornwall in May sometime? Perhaps I could discuss it with James this evening, would he agree to my going alone? Certainly he would not be very keen on the idea, but I was determined to go. I just had to go on my own, then I would know for certain whether the spirit would follow or not.

I vaguely heard James turning the light switch on and off.

"The electricity must have gone off," he muttered. "Damn and blast that is all we need, where did we put the torch, do you remember?" He was already striding towards the cupboard under the stairs, hearing him trip over something as he did so, and swear yet again.

At last a beam of light entered the hall. "I'll find the candles next and light them. It looks as though we are going to be without heat for a while. I wonder how long it will go on for, not long I hope as it is going to get extremely cold."

"Once you have lit the candles I will borrow the torch to go and fetch some blankets from upstairs, then at least we can cuddle into them and keep ourselves warm." I felt cool already, and shivered, tucking my hands up my sleeves for extra warmth.

Within a short while, we had candles lit, blankets on the settee, a bottle of wine, and some huge helpings of homemade fruit cake on the table by the side of it. "Can you think of anything else James before I settle down?"

"Yes let's have a look out the back door first to see how much more snow we have had since we last came in." The door was flung open to see the snow piled up high against the step, the snowflakes so large that they seemed to glisten as they fell.

"How magical it all looks," I whispered. "I do so love it when it's like this." I felt a nudge against my legs, knowing full well that it was Holly, wondering if her luck was in for another walk. I stood outside for a few minutes longer feeling strangely at peace. James had already gone in, but still I stayed on the doorstep. I seemed fascinated by the snow swirling down; it made me feel so sleepy.

For some unknown reason, I found myself whispering, "Leave us alone, go to the light with our love, we do not want you here, please go now, and do not return ever again." I really felt as though at that moment the spirit was there beside me. I felt suddenly very sad. I could feel tears slowly creeping down my cheeks. It felt as though a hand touched my hair, then lightly stroke my cheek, but this time it was not sinister, it was as though I were in a trance, I just wanted to stay there, perhaps that is what the spirit wanted, to keep me there in the freezing cold until I could feel no more. I remained there, my eyes now focusing on the snowflakes in the sky swirling and swirling down they came, faster and faster. My body suddenly felt weary and tired. In the distance I heard a voice, but it sounded so very far away, so distant, yet a voice I knew. "Catherine what the devil are you doing outside, you will get frozen if you keep out there any longer, whatever is it, why are you still out there?"

I whispered again to the spirit, "Go, go now, we don't want you here, go," my voice rising as I did so.

A hand grabbed mine, and I jumped. "For goodness sake come in now this instant Catherine, whatever is the matter with you, can't you hear me?" With that last command, I felt James pulling me back inside the safety of the kitchen. "Did you not hear me calling you?" he gasped, "and who were you talking too?"

I felt James half pull and half drag me to the settee. I heard something being poured into a glass and the next minute I felt a burning liquid being poured down my throat. I spluttered and choked, then heard a voice again, but louder this time.

"It's whisky Catherine, for goodness sake are you ill? Tell me, tell me now." His voice was rising again; I could tell he was getting hysterical like me. Still I did not answer until once again, I felt some more burning hot liquid being poured down my throat. It wasn't until I felt my dog's head in my lap that I started to be aware of where I was. I heard a voice which sounded very far away, but which really was mine, saying weakly, "Someone has died in this house, I can feel it, I can sense it." Slowly my eyes started to clear and I gradually began to focus. Dimly I saw the armchairs, a table, bookshelves full of books, a scarf and some wine. It was not until I saw my dog that I suddenly came too, and realised what had happened.

I felt strained as though drained of energy. My face felt sticky and cold. Someone had been out there with me, but I hadn't been frightened, and I was not afraid now, I just felt a deep feeling of bewilderment.

"James, I whispered, I just wanted to keep out there, it was so peaceful and beautiful for some unknown reason, that I'm sure I'll never know." My hands suddenly started to shake violently, then the shivers started and I could not stop trembling.

I saw the logs on the fire smouldering and heard the ash falling quietly into the grate; the candles flickered, as though a hidden draught came from somewhere. I felt James's arm go around me. "Come on love, you're tired, perhaps it was all in your imagination, you have been stressed out of late. The electric will be back on soon, then things will look brighter. I'm sure nothing was out there, it's all in your mind." He paused. "Things will seem a lot better after a good night's sleep." James scratched his head. "I must admit I did not feel anything at all out there, and Holly did not even bark or growl. I am sure she would have got agitated if the spirit had been about, she usually does. You're just over-exhausted that's all."

I nodded a tearful "yes" in reply, and sank even further down into the settee, snuggling into the blanket for comfort. I knew, just really knew, that someone had been out there with me, but best to go along with James for the moment, let him think that I'm just a tired and emotional female, over-reacting to the slightest thing.

I heard him moving about, fumbling slightly in the darkness of the room. Saw him stoop to bend down, picking up a patchwork blanket, and gently tuck it around me.

"Come on love, let's make the most of this, it is not often we have the chance of being all nice and snug in a cottage with a gale force blizzard raging outside. We could be without electricity for hours yet; at least we have the wood burner to keep this room warm so that we won't freeze. Are you feeling any better now, as I can't see your face in this candlelight, only the tip of your nose?"

I was feeling much more cheerful by this time, and with a voice that sounded surprisingly steady and strong, I said, "I'm fine now James thank you. I just feel so sorry for worrying you, you're right, I'm just over-tired as you say, let's have some delicious cake and wine, and make the most of it as you suggested."

We ate our homemade cake slowly, savouring the scent of the logs burning and the gentle heat coming from them. They were burning well. They smelt of pine wood that we had gathered from the forest in the summer. They reminded me of long walks when the weather had been warmer and kinder, bringing back the lovely aroma of pine trees, they smelt so gorgeous, the scent made me feel very relaxed and contented.

Our cake eaten, I realised that I still felt hungry. "Do me a favour James, look and see if there are any crisps or biscuits in the cupboard, or better still what about a crisp sandwich?"

"I'll see what I can find, but there is not much light in the kitchen, don't nag at me if I drop crumbs everywhere." With that he heaved his bulk out of the armchair, and ambled towards the kitchen.

Crash I heard a knife fall onto the kitchen floor, then another. "You're doing well," I called out, "don't bother if you can't see well enough, shall I come in and help?"

"No don't you dare, you just sit there and behave yourself, I don't want any more queer turns from you today, now just relax and have a little sleep while I get this tea sorted out. I'll be as quick as I can."

Tea eaten, it wasn't until several hours later when the candles were flickering dangerously low that I dare raise the issue of going to Cornwall on my own. I remembered that I had mentioned it to James a while back, but everything had been talked about rather vaguely, so I was feeling rather unsure of his reactions. I knew though that my mind was made up, whatever James said, I was going and that was that, end of story.

Nervously I put the question forward. I should have put it tactfully, but instead I blurted it out. "James in May I'm going to go to Cornwall for two weeks on my own. If the spirit follows me there, it will follow even if we move elsewhere. I must do it on my own otherwise we will never know."

"We have discussed this before Catherine as you well know, and I am not at all happy with it, but if you must go then you will, whatever I say. I can't stop you if your mind is made up."

With that a sudden blast of light lit up the room and thankfully eased the tension that had suddenly appeared between us.

"Thank goodness that has come back on. It has been six hours now since the electricity went off, soon it will be time for bed." He looked at me shrewdly. "Have you booked this holiday yet, and where are you going to stay?"

"I'm hoping to book it sometime this week, as the cottages get booked so quickly. It's in Boscastle just near the harbour so there are always plenty of people around. I'll take Holly as well so she will keep me company and let me know if anyone is about, but I'm positive that it will not be able to follow me. How can it all that way? It's just not possible. I know that you would like to come, but I must test this on my own. If I'm scared or it follows me I'll know straight away, and I promise that I will immediately come back home. I need a rest anyway. It will do us both good to have time on our own for a while. You have still got several months to get used to the idea of me being away with the dog. You will probably love it once I have gone, anyway. I'll book the cottage this week when I'm at work, then there will be no turning back. You know I must go on my own so the sooner it's done the better, though I don't know how Emma is going to take it, she will think it most odd that we are not going together."

James by this time was already clearing the bits and bobs away. Candles had been put in their boxes in the cupboard, blankets on the stairs ready to go up into the bedroom, plates and glasses were already being put into the kitchen. An odd silence had sprung up between us again which I could not seem to penetrate. Perhaps it was time for bed. It would give James time to accept it; there was no other way.

Before bed, we looked outside once more. This time I did not feel anything, just the bitter cold wind that the snow had brought. It was all silent and still now, no more snow tonight. It looked as though we would have a problem to reach work in the morning. The snow had been so heavy the roads would take a while to be cleared; already the thought of a duvet day was lurking in my mind. Perhaps it was time to have a day off from work for a change.

A hand touched me on the shoulder. "Let's go in now Catherine, I have had enough for one night. Go ahead and book your cottage in Cornwall, I don't like the idea at all, but realise that you must go. I'm now off to bed, goodnight." I heard him go into the kitchen, then up the stairs, no kiss before he went, nothing, things did not feel right between us now. This spirit was becoming a nuisance and I wondered sometimes if it were trying to split us up. Tiredness – thinking again, I must snap out of all this thinking of the spirit, and concentrate on positive things like booking my holiday, and spending more time with Emma and Adam. I seemed to have neglected them both lately.

I automatically locked the front door, kissed Holly who was already fast asleep in her bed, and turned the lights out, then slowly went up the stairs to bed feeling utterly dejected and exhausted. Our bedroom light was off, and the door slightly ajar, a positive sign that James was not happy. Oh! well another day tomorrow, perhaps things would seem happier in the morning.

I crept quietly into our room and into bed. James did not stir, or else he did not want to. That night seemed endless, I just could not sleep; time passed slowly, it must have been in the early hours of the morning when I finally drifted off into an uneasy doze.

I eventually awoke to the smell of burnt sausages, and turned tiredly over in bed. Sausages, what day was it, Sunday, no must be Monday, time for work. No I remembered now I was going to phone in sick, why, the snow perhaps. My mind completely muddled must have still been half asleep, when the bedroom door opened and a head poked round the door.

"It's been snowing heavily again during the night, this back road is completely blocked, so that means the main roads will not be clear with this snow for ages." I went to spring out of bed. "Keep in bed woman, I have already rung your office and told them that you cannot get in owing to the weather, so you might as well make the most of it. I'm doing a cooked breakfast for us both, can you smell it?"

I lay back in bed and grinned. "Gosh yes, breakfast in bed, what a treat, I cannot remember the last time this happened, it must have been ages ago, when the children were tiny." I was already beginning to feel hungry. What a kind thought of James.

"I'll bring it up in about ten minutes, bye."

With that his head disappeared from view. My watch said nine thirty. I really had over slept, but due to my bad night I must have needed it.

Slowly I pulled the duvet cover off, then walked quietly to the window and pulled back the curtains to see that everywhere was covered in several feet of snow. Icicles were hanging from the shed roof, everywhere looked silent and still with not a bird or creature in sight. It all looked so beautiful. I started to shiver with cold so crept back into bed to wait for my breakfast. My mind started to buzz with thoughts. I had been hoping for certain letters to arrive today, but I could not see the postman delivering any this morning. What a pity, never mind perhaps they would come in the morning.

The morning went quickly; it made a change for James and I to be together on our own for so long. We were both usually dashing off somewhere on our own in different ways. We had lunch and did the usual chores, until it was late afternoon.

"What are you up to now?" asked James peering over my shoulder.

"I'm looking through these brochures for somewhere to stay when I go on holiday to Cornwall. There are two on the harbour which look rather nice, perhaps I will ring up this afternoon, before it gets too late. It's already March, and they always seem to get booked up so quickly. I have decided to go in May, I'll try for the third week as hopefully it will be a little warmer by then, it's only two months away."

I saw James face twist up in displeasure. "Okay Catherine I suppose you know what you're doing, but I'm not happy with the idea at all as you very well know." He withdrew to his book. I suddenly felt alone; tension had arisen between us again. This spirit was not doing our marriage any good at all; the sooner I got this holiday over with the better. I picked the brochure up and went slowly towards the phone. "Yes could you book it for two weeks, the middle of May will be excellent, I'll put the deposit in the post first class in the morning, thank you so much." I banged the phone down, then went in search of my other half.

"I have booked it," I shouted out. Already I was beginning to look forward to a few weeks on my own, just with my dog for company. I had several friends who lived near where I would be staying in Boscastle, so it would be pleasant to see them all again.

We both returned to work the next day, each arriving at our respective jobs late. Snow was still piled up everywhere, making the roads icy and treacherous.

Emma rang that night in a tearful state to say she had skidded into a ditch that morning. No one was hurt, but her little Fiesta car which she drove, had been quite badly damaged in the front, where it had hit a tree. At least it took James's mind off my Cornish holiday. He worshipped his daughter, and would gladly do anything for her, even to the extent of buying her a new car, if necessary.

The snow gradually cleared, leaving lots of slush and wet about, which I hated. The weather got warmer, but it seemed to rain every day, which was most depressing. Oddly enough there was no trace of the presence after my encounter in the courtyard that night.

I would sometimes go into the study at night in the dark, and sit there waiting for a while, but strangely nothing ever came until thankfully, I started to forget about it all.

The month of May came round surprisingly quickly. "Why are you going on your own mum?" demanded Emma one afternoon. "Is there anything wrong between you and dad?" she queried. "You usually both go together, there must be something wrong."

Emma had kept probing these last few weeks, but I had been determined that she would not find out the real reason for my tour alone.

"I just want a break on my own Emma, I'm feeling rather tired at the moment, and feel like a complete rest. It will do me good so please do stop worrying."

Emma's lip pouted, knowing full well that I was spinning her a story.

"Oh well if you're not going to tell me don't, I won't bother asking anymore." With that Emma flounced out of the kitchen.

I gave a sigh and followed.

CHAPTER 4

JOURNEY TO CORNWALL

At long last the time came for me to be off.

I loaded the car up as quickly as I could. Trying hard to pack everything neatly, my biggest problem was that I always took far too much: jumpers, skirts, coats, blouses, shorts, trousers, boxes of food, nearly all of which would probably return back home with me, unworn and untouched, but then that was me. The morning of my departure was bright and clear. I kissed James goodbye and felt a slight tinge of sadness that he was not coming with me. Holly was getting all excited in the back of my ancient estate car, anxious to be off like me.

I drove off down the pathway to the gate, glancing at the study window as I did so, perhaps half expecting to see the presence looking out at me, but nothing was there.

I drove for what seemed a long time, until I sensed Holly getting restless. Luckily I was now passing through a quiet pretty little village, so changing gear I gradually slowed down to stop near a pleasant country lane. After a little break and exercise for us both, we headed off again. Time passed quickly. It grew hot in the car as it was now well into the afternoon. The signpost showed that I was now approaching Exeter. I opened the car window even further. Holly was now settled into a deep sleep, tired out after having had several walks along the way.

I now felt utterly relaxed and happy, the vibes coming out of me were saying: no work and no James, just me and my dog. I could do just what I wanted with only me to please. The warm air rushing through the window already smelt cleaner and fresher, my spirits rose again. I just knew that I was going to enjoy this holiday, and nothing was going to happen to spoil it; the spirit would not follow me, it was not able too.

Whether that was wishful thinking or not, only time would tell, at least I had my dog to protect me, or at least to let me know if anything was lurking about.

Now on the last lap of my journey I was feeling much more excited. I started to travel down narrow, twisty country lanes. I then caught my first sight of the sea, bringing back nostalgic memories of when the children were tiny. We used to love coming to Cornwall in those early years of our marriage. In fact in those days, we used to come down every single year, we loved it so much it was like our second home.

My memory went even further back into the past, to when whoever spotted the sea first would always win a whole pound to spend. I'm pretty positive that my daughter always cheated and won.

I could now clearly see the harbour of Boscastle nestling below me; I put the car into a low gear, and steered gently down the steep winding hill, passing quaint little houses covered with flowing colourful wisteria and ivy as I gradually descended. At last I reached the bottom without mishap, and parked the car near the cottage. Much to my delight my ears picked out the sound of a stream nearby, such a soothing, peaceful sound, which I always loved to hear. I hoped that I could listen to it from my bedroom window at night; it would help lull me to sleep.

It took me a long while to unload everything. Holly had been taken for yet another walk, and I had already found somewhere not far away that sold delicious chips, which I always adored at any time of the day.

It was by now getting late, and all the shops were shut, but by peering through the windows I could see that it would not take long to get rid of my spending money. There were shops galore full of eye catching crafts, pottery and candles, which I simply cannot resist. If by any chance it should rain in the morning, I knew exactly where I would be sheltering.

It had been a long day, and I suddenly felt and looked exhausted, so I then turned back to return to my cottage and bed.

I turned the key in the lock, and felt so glad that I had my dog with me. It felt lonely and it was growing dark quickly. It felt stuffy in the cottage, so I wearily climbed the stairs to open the bedroom window. I could hear the stream outside which instantly made me relax and feel more at ease. The night felt chilly, so I speedily ran a bath, and then went to bed.

My bed was comfortable but sleep did not come easily, every creak and noise seemed to alert me. The fact was that I was nervous, no doubt about that at all, though I felt certain that it was me being there all on my own. I was not used to being by myself at night in an empty cottage, it was all in my mind, and it was working overtime, I was sure of that.

It was no good, the minutes were ticking steadily by, I just could not drift off. My brain just would not stop thinking. Suddenly making my mind up, I jumped out of bed. I would do a forbidden thing, go and fetch Holly from downstairs. She could sleep on the bed with me every night. Why had I not thought of that earlier?

Holly was so pleased to be with me you could see her thinking, oh to be up on the bed with mother, what fun.

Funnily enough once she was with me, I relaxed and fell straight away into a deep sleep, not waking up until eight in the morning, which was late for me. I felt something nudging my hand, my eyes then slowly focused on Holly, who nudged me yet again. Food, time to get up, she seemed to be saying, hurry up, but much to her disappointment I just could not stir. My limbs felt so relaxed and comfortable as though I were in another world. Thinking back, I had not felt like that for a long time. Was it because I was away from the spirit, was it secretly draining me at home, could it not reach me here, was that why I was feeling so much better this morning?

Drifting gently in and out of sleep, I remembered that I must ring James today, to let him know I had arrived safely, and that so far the spirit had not appeared. No doubt he would be expecting me to ring him each day, but I decided that I wouldn't; I needed a complete break away from everything and everyone on the home front.

At last I made myself get up to have a lazy breakfast, but when you own a dog, that is often quite impossible, which it proved to be, the sun was shining, so I did not hesitate for long.

Packing a light lunch, a flask and bowl of water for Holly, then with light footsteps, I closed the front door with a bang and headed for the cliffs. I could not wait to get my first glimpse of the sea and cliffs again. My mind searched back to when I had last visited Cornwall. It must have been three years ago, no wonder I had been missing it. What an age ago it all seemed, it made me realise how busy and stressful life had become. Within five minutes I had reached the little church. I slowly opened the heavy swing gate, only to have to shut it firmly again after me. The churchyard was old with many graves going back several centuries but for once I did not even glance at them. It was the cliffs that I wanted today. So with eagerness I headed through the second and last little gate which led to the cliffs and pastures beyond.

Holly hesitated and looked to me for comfort. This was unknown territory for her. She was used to the woods and chasing after pine cones and sticks. This was a wilderness of little patches of green and grey looking fields set out like a patchwork quilt in the early morning sun, running on for miles and miles, all sloping down until you came to the cliff walks below. Once through the gate I saw the sea in the distance, how marvellous it all looked. Hastening my speed, I headed towards it, breathing in the lovely clean fresh sea air, feeling my long hair blowing in the wind. This was good. I could see no one in sight which was better still. I enjoyed my own company; you could then do as you pleased, with no one to answer to. Memories were still coming flooding back to me. There should be a little seat somewhere nearby, perhaps a little further on. More or less running by now, I rounded the next bend. I gasped, I had completely forgotten how beautiful it all was. Beyond me were what must be some of the finest views in England – cliffs all rugged and full of gorse, winding like snakes through all the little inlets and coves for miles around, little tiny paths twisting and turning. Everywhere was so silent; all you could hear was the sea crashing on the rocks below. If only I could put all of this lovely view in my pocket and take it home with me to keep forever, how wonderful it would be. I found it quite a steep climb to the top and exhausting. I could feel the wind rushing through my hair, and the fresh breeze blowing in my face, it was marvellous. The wild view and ruggedness of the scenery brought a few tears to my eyes. It was so beautiful and I loved it. Walking along the little paths which were surrounded on either side with wild gorse, I could see the sea crashing far below on the rocks. Not a living soul was in sight; it was so wonderful that I could have stayed there forever. How I wished I could move to this part of the world.

"Come on Holly," I shouted, "we are going to walk all along these cliffs today until we reach Tintagel, then we will catch the bus back, and buy us a huge Cornish pasty for our tea. What do you think of that for a treat?" Her tail wagged to its full capacity in reply.

That night I slept soundly once again. True I had well and truly worn myself out with fresh air, walking and good food. Not only that, I felt contented and at peace, as though the presence was very far away, and beyond my reach. My thoughts were drifting further, would the spirit be waiting for me back at home, would it still visit without me there and await my return?

Another thought entered my head which disturbed me. I had not rung James today. How was he coping, was he missing me? I somehow doubted it. Things were just not quite right between us, and I was doubtful whether they would be so again.

How quickly I had adjusted to being on my own. Did I really love James? I now questioned it myself, and wondered.

The next morning I awoke earlier, to the sun once again streaming onto my bedroom, though instead of me being sleepy, it was my dog still thoroughly exhausted from yesterday's walking and adventures.

Gently I tried to creep out of bed without wakening her, but one eye opened instantly, then the other. That was it, she bounded off the bed. She was down even before my two feet had touched the floor.

The week passed quickly, all without mishap. My thoughts after that first night had not returned at all to think of the spirit that was shadowing me.

I had not even made contact with my friend who lived just outside Tintagel. I must do so and quickly. Only one more week left, it would go even faster than the first week, so much still to do, and time was running out.

My numerous outings had already explored all the quaint little craft shops round about, spending my hard earned money for presents to take home. My afternoon treat was to have a scone, filled with jam and cream, with my dog sleeping contentedly by my side, both of us watching the world go by.

It was on the tenth day that I felt decidedly on edge and for no apparent reason at all. The day had been more cloudy and chillier than usual, so I had returned to the cottage to have an afternoon of writing postcards, and to catch up on some reading. I had as usual brought with me far too many books and magazines, perhaps now was the time to catch up on some of them.

As soon as I entered the cottage I knew that something was there waiting for my return; my hair suddenly started to prickle, I stiffened, and Holly did not want to come in.

I glanced at my watch, it was only early afternoon, but for some odd reason the lounge was already in near darkness. My eyes went towards the kitchen where it looked much lighter, which meant that my feelings were correct; the presence was here in the lounge with me, probably at this very moment watching my every move.

My eyes then turned towards the stairs. I felt as though it was willing me to go up them and my heart was thumping loudly, I could hear it.

Something touched my legs. I heard myself gasp, or was it a scream. In one single glance, I saw that it was Holly, faithful as always to be by my side, against her instincts she had decided to follow me in.

Nervously, I looked round again, the presence I felt was still there. Oddly enough I could not smell it this time, but somehow I knew that it was there in the shadows. Just hovering and waiting, but why and for what, there must be some reason. Thoughts were entering my head that it wanted me back at home and quickly. How could it put thoughts inside my head, or was it already part of me in some way that I did not know? I knew this time that it did not want to hurt me, only to know that I was safe and it wanted me to go back home.

My knees felt oddly weak, I must sit down. Grabbing at the nearest chair I gratefully sank into it.

Why after ten days of being in this cottage alone, did this spirit suddenly appear out of nowhere? My brain just could not fathom it out at all. Holly was still very unsettled and restless. She kept very close to me just like a shadow, making me even more nervous.

Quickly my arm reached out to the light switch. I must have light, yes that was the answer, put them all on everywhere. I knew that for some reason the presence did not like the light. That would make it go away.

Hesitantly my body stopped at the bottom of the stairs, knowing full well that I must go up them to the top. I must have the light on in every room.

Nervously my legs started to climb them, slowly at first then more quickly as I gained strength and courage.

The bedroom window had blown wide open, making the room feel cold and chilly. As I reached out to shut it, the curtain flapped into my face making me scream. Pushing it wildly away, I ran for the light switch tripping over the edge of the carpet in my rush to do so.

My fingers started to grovel for the switch; I must have light. At last my trembling fingers found it. Not even bothering to look round I sped down the stairs to the kitchen. Coffee, I must have some coffee, I would feel better in the kitchen where it was brighter. My hands shakily put the kettle on. A few minutes passed while it came to the boil, but it was no good, I must get out of the cottage for a while, now this very minute. Hopefully it would be gone by the time I got back, and not return.

I shook myself in bewilderment, was I imagining all of this, or had the spirit really got into my head. My instincts told me that it was here with me though not in a sinister way.

Not waiting to think any more, I quickly grabbed my bag, along with Holly's lead and my keys. Not looking back, I fled towards the door and out.

My arm crashed against the door in my rush to get out, making my eyes glisten with unshed tears, my body feeling tense and stressed. Oh! why did this have to happen, I had been so happy and safe until this moment.

How on earth I reached the village of Zennor I just do not know, as I could not even remember the journey. My watch showed that it was now five in the afternoon, with the sun now shining once again. The journey in the car had taken a whole hour, but why had I taken the road to Zennor? My head ached, and my body felt drained, just too tired to think any more about it, for a while anyway. My head rested against the car window for a while, until my person felt more like its usual self again. The scenery outside looked pretty; perhaps it would be wise to go and find somewhere to eat first. There must be a pub in the nearby vicinity.

A couple with arms linked together strolled by. Making a grab for my purse I decided to follow them. Sure enough after about ten minutes they led me to the prettiest pub you could imagine. The smell of good hot food filled my nostrils, making me feel terribly hungry. From within came the cheerful sound of laughter and noise. This was what I needed to take my mind of other things, and to stop me thinking too much.

Several hours later, with my strength and humour fully restored, I returned to the car to make my journey steadily back to the cottage, and to whatever awaited me there.

As my vehicle moved off, I wondered again if everything had been in my imagination, but something had been there earlier on, which had made me feel so nervous. My dog had felt it as well, I was sure of it.

Looking at my watch yet again – seven thirty – too late now to ring up James. I would make certain that I would speak to him first thing in the morning, just to see if he had been visited by the presence at all in my absence.

By the time I finally arrived back at the cottage it was late. My eyes immediately went to the windows; they were all ablaze with the lights, which I had left on earlier. I felt pensive again, missing James for the second time since I had been away. I saw Holly wagging her tail, and I brightened.

At least I had my dog. I wasn't really alone and with that firmly in my mind I trudged wearily towards the cottage.

Once inside I took a quick look around; it felt empty. Holly came bounding in, happily scrounging around for missed crumbs on the floor as always.

By now I was feeling much more relaxed, though still slightly on edge, listening for the slightest sound. Whatever had been there had gone, though some instinct deep inside me, told me that the presence was not far away. That night I slept uneasily. A candle, which I had put on my bedside table kept flickering as though a hidden draft was coming from somewhere. I blew the candle out. It was making too many ghostly shadows. My body lay rigid in bed for a few minutes trying very hard not to feel agitated, but it was not any good. I lit the candle once again. I could not be without light. I then fell into a fitful restless sleep.

The morning came at last, with the dawn chorus deafening to my ears. I had not slept very well at all. My eyes felt bleary and heavy with sleep. Ponderously my mind started to think. Immediately after breakfast I would ring James before he set off to the college for work.

The phone booth smelt musty and damp. Quickly I dialled his number. I could hear the phone ringing and ringing for what seemed to be ages. James must be at home; it was far too early for him to leave for work yet. Perhaps he was ill.

My thoughts were now racing, uneasy feelings creeping into my head, as I banged the telephone down.

The sun suddenly broke through the clouds promising a warm day, which was too good to be missed wasting time in a telephone booth. If anything had been wrong at home, James would have been in touch somehow. Time enough when I arrived back after my holidays to question why had he been out at that time of the morning.

The morning air smelt so wonderfully fresh and clean, I could smell the salt air from the sea and hear the crashing of waves on the rocks in the far distance.

I had already made up my mind, that the upset of yesterday was not going to spoil the last few days of my holiday. Deep down I had the feeling that the presence would not return again while I was in Cornwall. Why I felt that I just could not say. I only knew that I would not sense it again until I returned home.

That same day I decided to visit a couple of friends who lived in the next village to Boscastle, friends whom I had known for years.

Luckily they were in. It turned out that it was just what I needed to lift my spirits – lots of laughter and gossip followed by a delicious lunch. The time went so quickly and all too soon I was saying my goodbyes, promising to see them again next year. My day as always ended up walking along the cliff tops, seeing for the first time a real live badger, which made me feel so excited.

By the time I returned to the cottage, myself and the dog were completely worn out. It had been a good day, a long one but a good one.

The evening was pulling in. I drew the curtains hastily across the windows making the cottage look cosy and warm, my dog already curled up and fast asleep on the rug. Evidently the presence was not about at the moment.

Sleepily I wandered into the kitchen to make myself a nightcap, before heading upstairs to bed. The clock in the hall chimed loudly making me jump. It was getting late. Still feeling slightly apprehensive, I took one last look around before I finally succumbed to bed and hopefully sleep.

The bed felt cosy and warm, with the gurgle of the brook outside. I drifted off into a dreamless sleep.

The next thing I knew was that it was late morning. I had slept long and heavily, waking up to a morning that looked bright and promising. Lazily I counted the days left of my holiday. Only three more to go, time was going far too quickly. Despite the happenings of yesterday, I did not wish to return home.

I had enjoyed my time in Cornwall; it was a pity I had to go back.

The last few days fled by. All I seemed to do was eat all my favourite things like chips and fudge, and walk along the cliffs which I knew and loved so much, taking the opportunity to sit in a sheltered pretty spot for a while, watching the sea pound on the rocks far below, or to just read and chill out. One day before I was due to go back, there was a decidedly cool nip in the air, perhaps a change in the weather. It would therefore be wise for me to have the day on the cliffs, in case it rained in the morning.

With sinking feelings, I gathered my bits together, knowing it was near to the end of my two weeks' stay. Half an hour later, I was on my way to the cliffs, with Holly running with boundless energy ahead. I hadn't gone far when I slowly retraced my footsteps. I must first ring James, try and catch him in for once. I hesitated – something wanted me to make that call to him, though deep down I didn't really want too.

Turning the next corner, my eyes alighted on a phone box and knew that I must make the call. Commonsense told me that I should do so; James would otherwise be cross when I got home if I didn't ring. I had only spoken to him once in two weeks, which was not very good.

My mind finally made up, I half dragged and pulled Holly into the phone booth with me, how she hated them, and squeezed inside.

This time James picked up the phone instantly, his voice sounding welcoming and pleased to hear that I was enjoying myself, but inwardly I felt there was something he wanted to say to me, but did not know how, or was I imagining it?

"Is there something wrong James, please tell me if there is?" I felt a pause for a moment; the phone seemed to go dead. I waited feeling my chest tightening, knowing full well that something fresh had happened.

"Yes something has happened." James fell silent again. My hands tapped the phone impatiently.

"Come on, tell me, has the spirit been about again? Are you ill? Has something been going on? What is it, you must tell me now, my voice rising higher with each sentence. James tell me, tell me now what is it."

For endless minutes there was dead silence.

The voice of James now sounded so different to the one I knew and used to love, it sounded distant but somehow vague.

"Something happened a few nights ago, several things in fact; things that you will find hard to believe, things that I cannot really say over the phone. It is best if I tell you when you are safely back home, it will only make you nervous if I do. I'll tell you when I see you, bye."

Before I could reply, the telephone went dead. James had hung up. Whatever had been going on? He had sounded odd, distant, as though he did not really want me to return home.

Miserably I stared at the silent phone. I felt Holly's tongue lick my hand, knowing that she wanted to be outside, but still I did not move. What was it, had the spirit been haunting James while I had been away? Had some other mischief been occurring in my absence, whatever could it be?

Holly nudged my hand this time, but harder. In a despondent mood I opened the door, feeling the freshness of the morning on my hot cheeks. The wind had picked up whilst I had been speaking to James and the sun had gone in behind dark clouds in the sky. It looked like rain, possibly that was why my spirits had mysteriously sunk to a very low level, or was it the thought of home, so very near now? Only one more day to go before I went from this lovely peaceful environment, to whatever lay ahead back in Shropshire.

Still feeling miserable, I decided to spend the rest of the day looking round the shops, spending my last few precious pennies on presents and last minute bits and pieces, making me overspend on my budget as usual, which I had been determined for once to keep. Holidaymakers just arriving made me feel envious so that I felt bad tempered and tearful. Tomorrow Saturday would be my very last day, even Holly would miss all the wonderful days with me along the North Coast, chasing rabbits and eating half of my Cornish pasty most days. How I spoilt that dog, I loved her so much.

It grew dark early that night. The clouds darkened and there was no moon in sight. A storm seemed to be brewing, and the cottage did not seem quite at ease. It was restless as though things were still to come. Fortunately I fell asleep quickly, not bothering for once to light the candle that I now kept flickering throughout the night.

I awoke with a sinking feeling in the pit of my stomach; my ears could hear the rain lashing at the windows, the wind whistling around the cottage. My final day and it was raining – just my luck. As it was my last day, what could I do, walking would be hopeless in this storm, and the change in the weather made the cottage feel ominous and creepy.

After a subdued breakfast I decided to take Holly for a short run first; then return back to the cottage to slowly start packing; then possibly have a good pub lunch somewhere locally, do any

79

last minute shopping; then leave for home in the region of late evening and travel back through the night. For some reason I couldn't fathom out, I now didn't want to stop another night. It felt different as though something were about to happen.

My decision made, I felt better. I would let James know this evening when I was on my way home, that I would arrive early in the morning. That way there would be no arguments about me travelling through the night on my own.

By the time I had finished packing and tidying up, it was well into the afternoon. I seemed as though I was becoming more and more agitated by the minute. I really felt as though the presence was going to visit me again, my instincts felt certain of it. I must go and quickly, my nerves were on edge. I must go, get out now, something inside my inner self was telling me that things were not right, to go now. Rushing briefly into every room checking that I had left nothing behind, I rushed out, slamming the door behind me. I pushed the suitcases and Holly quickly into the car, the rain lashing the windows as I hurriedly drew away, taking one glance at the cottage as I did so, with a mixture of regret at leaving it and fear of the unknown which I felt would make itself known tonight as soon as darkness appeared.

The journey had been long and tiring. I had only made two stops on the journey to keep me awake, but night driving is tedious and boring, even Holly had not stirred when I had pulled in to have a break at a service station, or to fill up with petrol. The motorways were nearly empty of traffic, just a few haulage trucks along the way, making the driving even more monotonous and boring. I missed the views; some parts had been so pretty on the way up. In the darkness you could see nothing, which in turn made you feel bored, so that I was constantly reaching for some sweets to pass the time away, which in turn made me feel sick.

Eventually as dawn was breaking, and with much relief, I saw the signs for Shropshire. I had driven a long way, and now I just wanted to be home, and put my head down on a nice soft pillow. Whatever it was that lay ahead, I was now ready to tackle what might be waiting.

By the time I arrived home it was still only six in the morning, too early to go in and possibly disturb James in doing so. The morning appeared dry and warmish. If I took the dog for a run in the woods for about an hour it would then be about the right time to go indoors and show my face.

Everywhere looked and felt flat against the North Coast of Cornwall; it would take me quite a few days to settle back into a routine. I had become accustomed to lazy breakfasts and only my dog for company, which I had enjoyed immensely. What a change from the life I had left behind. Deep down I knew that I had not wanted to return to the cottage that I called home.

Holly was at least happy to be home again. I had parked the car a few doors away from the cottage, that way I would not disturb James who at this early hour would still be asleep.

She knew where she was straight away and ran the few yards on her own up to the entrance of the road, which took you to the woods beyond.

I could smell the pine trees in the faint breeze, making everything seem so relaxed. Was there really a spirit or presence, which was following me?

On this calm misty morning it was hard to believe that there were such things, even harder to know that it was I who was the source of the presence coming at all.

My walk through the nearby woods helped me considerably; I used to take the children down here when they were younger. In those days we had a Springer Spaniel who used to bound and run everywhere, the family used to adore her, but now was the time to head back for home.

I slowly stepped round to turn back, my footsteps now considerably slower with each step that I took. I did not want to go back, I wanted to be back in Cornwall on my own with my dog. Somehow I knew that I was just making things hard for myself. I was afraid of this presence, spirit, ghost, force. Whatever this thing was it seemed further away in Cornwall than here in Shropshire. Or was it James that I really did not want to come back to. Had I come to a stage in my life when I needed pastures new, or was I just frightened of the unknown?

James had been strange on the phone. Was there a reason or was he just tired of everything? He had not liked me going on holiday alone without him.

I was nearly home now. Holly knew where she was, running up the little road with her tail wagging, stopping outside the right gate to go in.

CHAPTER 5

RETURN HOME

There was no escape now; I was standing at my own front gate. I had no choice but to go in. The dog was happy enough to be home, so possibly it was me just getting over-tired and being silly. I could smell the honeysuckle as I walked through the gate; it made me feel better.

James was already up by the time I had let myself in the door. He looked pleased to see me, but with a slight hesitancy, which had not been there before.

"Welcome home my dear it's lovely to see you again." His voice sounded rather formal, as though he had better things to do, or was it perhaps my imagination working at full force once again. I knew that I was tired from the long journey and possibly over reacting to the situation, but nonetheless I stored it away in my mind to ponder over much later on.

"I'm exhausted now from the long car journey through the night, but the holiday was wonderful. I feel so much more rested." Fondly I glanced at him, "I did miss you though, lots and lots." There was silence. I looked again at him. He was not paying any attention to me; he seemed as if he had other things on his mind.

Perhaps he had. My mind started to wonder. Had he found himself another woman? Surely not we were too close for that. Was it work, or worry over something that I did not know about?

"It seemed odd without you, but I soon got used to it, and I have returned so much more rested." I looked again at his face; I could see that he was not really listening to me, but was deep in thought.

Bending down he did manage to make a small fuss of the dog, but even that was short-lived, he was not really a doggie person. Barely glancing at me, his hand reached for the kettle. "Coffee as usual I presume?" Already James was putting the mugs out on the table, not even waiting for me to answer. "I have cleaned and hoovered all up for you, so that you can take it easy today. Emma and Adam might come over late this afternoon, though I did tell them that you might need a sleep first after driving all that long way on your own. Why you drove all that way through the night is beyond my reasoning. Much better to have travelled down early this morning I would have thought." His voice sounded cold and frosty.

I sat myself down at the kitchen table, so that I could study the expression on James's face as he was talking. Dare I risk asking the question, which had been on my mind these last few days since my last telephone call to him?

"Has the spirit been here while I have been away? I desperately need to know."

His eyes narrowed and turned questionably towards me. "Has it been with you, tell me that first Catherine?"

My eyes diverted to the coffee that I was now stirring, seeing the milk winding deep down into the water, bubbles appearing on the top as I turned the spoon far to vigorously and fast, still hesitating not knowing really what to say. Should I tell him the truth, or to tell him a little white lie and pretend nothing had happened? I had never been any good at lying, so James would know at once. I thought it best to tell him everything.

"I don't really how to start, as it only happened the once, at the very end of my holiday. At the beginning I felt like a new person. I was just so convinced that it wouldn't and couldn't reach me so far away from home. I definitely could not feel it or smell it. It just was not there, my whole being was feeling so relaxed, that to tell you the truth I did not even think of it, all of the events seemed all so far away from my thoughts at that time."

My hand shook slightly. I held the warm cup of coffee more closely to me for comfort and carried on.

"It must have been in the region of the tenth day that it visited me, though I'm wondering now if it was all in my mind, as I didn't even smell it this time, no aroma at all."

James, I could see, was getting restless. "What made you think it was there?" he spoke impatiently. That in itself was unusual for him.

I shivered. The kitchen to me felt cold as though somebody else were listening. Did the spirit know that I was back? Was it waiting upstairs for me? James seemed to sense my sudden nervousness, as he remained quiet until I had composed myself.

"As I was saying it wasn't until well into the holiday that the spirit returned. I did not see it or smell it, I only had this

85

really deep feeling that the presence was there watching me for a while, even Holly was uneasy." I then went into detail of all that had happened that day.

James was looking at me in an odd way that I could not understand. I sat staring at my wedding finger on my hand, it felt loose. I must have lost some weight recently, still neither of us spoke. "It did come there the one time, on the tenth day I think, but I'm not certain, why is it so important to you?" I said anxiously.

"Do you remember what day it was? It's very important you tell me exactly when it was." It all came out in a rush as though he was desperate for an answer.

"I'm really sure about it, James. I felt as though it only came to see where I was and that I was safe. Don't ask me how I can know that, but I do. I'm certain now it can enter my thoughts if it wants to but that is all that happened. It was there I know it was and it frightened me at the time. Seriously though nothing else occurred, now over to you James, tell me what has been happening here."

"You're not going to believe what I'm going to tell you Catherine, even I keep turning it over and over in my mind. There is simply no other explanation. It must have been the presence making itself known to me while you have been away."

A silence penetrated the kitchen while James fumbled for fresh words.

"Since the first day you went off to Cornwall it has been here. Every time I have gone up the stairs it has been lurking. It seems to be mainly on the staircase landing that it waits and watches as though awaiting your return. It's been restless even I can feel that. It has been wanting you back that I do know, but that is not all." He stopped once again deep in thought. I glanced at James's face again. He looked more like his normal self, possibly the presence had been worrying him more that I had realised.

"Just start at the beginning, tell me everything as it has happened." My hand touched his for comfort. "Come on James start again please, I know it's not been easy but you must tell me." In the far distance amidst all the twittering of the other birds, I could hear a cuckoo calling. What a peaceful sound it made, as though everything was normal but it wasn't. Not here anyway, not at this moment of time. I felt James withdraw his hand from mine, heard him clear his throat.

"Alright I'll tell you everything from the beginning, as it happened, bit by bit, but you will find it hard to accept. I know I do, but it's the honest truth, all of it. I'm not making any of it up, I only wish I were." He paused to push his empty cup away.

"After you went on holiday that Saturday everything looked and appeared fine. It was a warm sunny day if you remember, so I spent most of it pottering outside in the garden. There was so much weeding to do after all that rain the week before. Adam came round that afternoon about five-thirty, so after a while we went down the pub for a pint. It was good to see the lad, we don't seem to have seen much of him of late." James then lapsed into a further silence, as though thinking of the events ahead. It took him several minutes to gain his thoughts together before resuming.

"Adam went home in the region of nine thirty, so I did the usual things like clearing away the tea things and locking up." His eyes focused on me intently. "To be truthful and with no disrespect to you Catherine, I had not thought of you once since you had left that morning. I had been so occupied and busy with other things, you know how it is. Once Adam had gone, I watched the news, made a last minute cup of tea before I took myself off to bed, with still no thought at all of this wretched presence or of you for that matter. I was tired, so all I wanted was to go to bed and sleep."

James closed his eyes for the moment in sheer concentration, and took a deep breath.

"I started to climb the stairs when I began to feel a strange sensation in my body. My head started to prickle and tingle. I then felt icy cold. Something lightly touched my neck, then my forehead, and every single hair on my body felt as though it were standing on end. I knew then that your ghost was now with me at that very moment on the landing at the very top of the stairs. I could smell it and feel it so very close to me it was threatening – as though waiting and wanting to push me down the stairs. I knew that I was now in great danger. How I knew that I don't know, perhaps animal instinct. Somehow I felt it was blaming me for your disappearance and it wanted to be rid of me. I felt it was speaking to me, saying over and over again: where is she? What have you done with her? I want her back now."

James gulped nervously as though not wanting to carry on. "I then saw it; I saw a shadow, a tall black shadow which was now standing at the top of the stairs. My whole being then froze with terror; it was I knew intent on pushing me down those stairs. It was very angry. You were not here Catherine. It wanted you and you only. The presence thought that I had sent you away, I'm absolutely certain of it." James's face was ashen as he carried on. "It was a terrifying experience Catherine, I ran to the bathroom downstairs slamming the door as hard as I could behind me. Running the cold tap over my face and hands to stop myself shaking like a leaf, before I was violently sick. That's how awful it all was." James took another deep breath and he took my hands gently into his own. "It seemed that I sat there for hours, I was just too frightened to go beyond that door, me a grown man of fifty, that's how sinister it all was.

"That is only the beginning, there is so much more. How I got away from it I just don't know. I dived back into the lounge, and slept on the settee until the morning. I have never felt so scared in all my life."

James's face was now white and visibly shaken. Even I was beginning to feel frightened. What else had happened in my absence? Things were far more serious than we had thought.

I sat motionless while James slowly composed himself; his voice was subdued as he attempted the next part of the story.

"I somehow knew that it might have been waiting up on the landing all night for me to go up those stairs. I felt as if it were putting thoughts into my mind, just like it does to you. That night was endless, at every slight sound I would freeze I was so scared that it was coming to get me, whatever it was. I just simply dare not go to sleep. It was silly really as it couldn't possibly do anything physical to me, how could it, a ghost, but nonetheless I was terrified and did not sleep a wink that night."

"In the morning things felt a lot brighter, as though back to normal, the presence had gone, or I felt that it had.

"It was Sunday, so I fried myself some breakfast and took it easy for a while, then walked along to the shop to get the usual Sunday newspaper. By late afternoon I was getting rather bored and fed up with myself, so I decided to clean the cooker for you as a pleasant surprise, I know how you hate that particular job." His eyes went to the kitchen clock, "It must have been around four in the afternoon when I started to clean the cooker, all thoughts of the presence had now gone completely from my head. I had even gone up the stairs earlier on to have a shower, but there was no sign of anything whatsoever. I had looked and smelt in every single room, just nothing there." Before going on, James reached out for a tissue, as though trying to gain time before his next sentence.

"It all happened so quickly. One minute I had my head bent in the oven, the next, I heard an almighty crash from upstairs. It sounded as though it was coming from the study; the noise was so loud, as if a brick had been thrown through the window. I tore up the stairs two at a time straight into the study. There in the middle of the floor sat your Italian bone china vase, the one that you have always loved so much. There was an overpowering smell of something vile in the room, so strong that it made me gasp, then to my utter horror I then saw a mist rising from where the vase was laying." James looked directly into my eyes. "Where did you leave that vase Catherine, I thought it always lived on the far corner shelf?"

"It does, it always lives on that shelf, but how on earth could it have landed in the middle of the floor? The vase sits on the shelf right at the end of the room. It must be a different vase that you are talking about James, come on, show me which one it was."

James went first up the stairs with me following closely behind and entered the study. "There I have left the vase exactly as it landed," his finger shook slightly as he pointed to it. "Is that the vase that usually sits over there?" Meekly I nodded my head as a yes. "Well how the devil could it get from there to right over here without breaking? The vase is so fragile that any slightest knock would break it, and if, and only if, it fell on its own accord, it would have just fallen off the shelf to the floor beneath. It certainly would not have landed halfway across the room with such a crash."

We stood silently in that room for several minutes, both our minds going over the things that had just been said, but with no answer to the mystery at all – only one more thing to be added to the list of strange happenings. I miserably went to the chair by the window and gazed out, looking down into the courtyard below.

I felt utter bewilderment. How could a fragile vase be thrown with such forcefulness across a room and not break? How did it get there? Was the presence a spirit or a force? I was still staring out of the window, when I heard James's voice rise. "How do you see it Catherine, how do you think it got there if it is not the force? Come on you must have some ideas about it; I know that I'm getting sick of the whole thing."

"I don't know any more than you do!" I shouted back. "Did anything else happen while I was away besides what you have told me today?"

"Only that it or whatever it is, was often up on the landing here, but I did not get that sinister feeling that I had before. Possibly it had found you in Cornwall safe, so that it was content enough to await your return. You still have not told me when the presence visited you in Cornwall. What time was it, do you remember, morning, afternoon?" His forceful probing brought me back to reality.

"I suppose it must have been late afternoon." My mind was trying hard to go back to that day, which to me seemed so far away now. All I could remember was that it was late afternoon; it looked as though both the happenings had more or less occurred at the same time.

His frown deepened. "We must get help somehow and soon, this just cannot go on." He too came to the window and looked out.

"But why is it so attached to me, James?" I had lost count of all the times I had thought and spoken those few words. What is the meaning of it all? My holiday now seemed so far away, a thing of the past. I was now back home to reality, with a vengeance, and I did not like it one little bit.

"First thing Monday morning I'll give the clairvoyant a ring to see if she can come over sooner. If I tell her it's really urgent I'm sure she will do her best." As I was speaking tears that had been lurking now started to overflow. I had so enjoyed my break away, now it was all being destroyed within a matter of a few hours.

I felt James pull me towards him. It was the old James back for a while, pulling me to him so that our bodies entwined for a while. His kiss was with longing and passionate as if we had our young years back again.

We forgot our worries for a little while. It was a pleasant interlude while it lasted. It made us feel closer as though a curtain had been slipped back into time.

By the time we eventually got downstairs, it was lunchtime. James now in a good humour said bravely, "While you unpack all your things, I will do us a light lunch, then for a special treat I'll cook dinner for you tonight."

Things now looked brighter for the future, and I felt optimistic. I was now back in tune again with James, at least for a while.

"You go and tidy yourself up, while I unpack your car for you." He was already striding through the back door in his eagerness to please me.

I smiled to myself. Perhaps things would be all right if there were two of us to tackle the problem, which we had.

Putting everything to the back of my mind, I reached for Holly's water bowl to refill it with fresh water, then eagerly climbed the stairs to have a shower. That would help waken me up after such a long journey. Before doing so I peeped into the study thinking that I would soon have to put new curtains up at the window, it needed fresh ones. These were old, tatty and dingy, that went way back from our past house in Essex. They had done well but were really very ancient. New ones would brighten things up, then perhaps a new carpet – that would make me feel better with the study.

My steps took me across the room to once again look down on the courtyard below – my thoughts still as far away from the spirit as you could possibly get – when out of thin air, or so it seemed at the time, I was engulfed in a swirling cobweb sort of mist, something like a sea mist that suddenly and very quickly creeps up on you silently and unawares out of the water. I smelt the ghastly scent, which I now knew and dreaded so much. The presence had come to welcome me back. It was telling me so. It was pleased that I had returned. These thoughts were being hammered into my head. It was talking to me, and it meant to stay.

It had all happened so unexpectedly, it was too much, I promptly burst into tears and ran out, slamming the door behind me as hard as I could, making up my mind at the same time, that I would not enter that room again until the clairvoyant had visited us.

Forgetting about my shower, I ran downstairs heading for the kitchen and James.

At precisely that moment, James walked through the back door heaving in my suitcase, shouting out, "What have you got in here Catherine it weighs an absolute ton, what sort of junk have you bought home this time?"

Silence followed, I just could not speak. "Whatever is the matter Catherine, what is it, what has happened?"

Another outbreak of tears burst from me. "It's here James, it's in the study, it just appeared from nowhere. It's letting me know that it's content now that I'm back. It wants to keep me here James. It's telling me in my head, somehow it's talking to me, I don't want it. We have got to get it to go away; it might make me go mad if it stays." I could hear my voice rising hysterically.

I wanted now more than anything else to go away from this cottage and never ever to return. "I want to move James and now!" Tears were now pouring down my cheeks uncontrollably, heartrending sobs breaking from my body. I could feel James gently seating me in the rocking chair, then sitting beside me.

"That won't do any good now will it, be sensible, just think a minute, it can now follow you if it wishes to. We must somehow lay it at rest so that it cannot torment or get into your head. There must be a way; we must not panic. That's just what it wants us to do. As we said earlier, you ring the clairvoyant first thing in the morning and get her over here as fast as she is able to, the presence only appears with you in the study, so keep out of there. Come on love cheer up. Think of your holiday in Cornwall. I'm sure the clairvoyant will be able to come over this week and do something about it. I'll go up the stairs now and run your bath for you, then after lunch we will pop over to Emma's, she is longing to see what you have bought her back from holiday, you know what she is like."

Wearily James sat on the edge of the settee. He could hear Catherine splashing about in the bath upstairs. Slowly he put his hand in his pocket and pulled out a worn leather wallet. Inside, folded up neatly, was a scrap piece of paper. On it was Amidyne's, the clairvoyant's, telephone number. Quietly he reached for the telephone, inwardly knowing that he shouldn't be ringing her on a Sunday, but he must. She had to come over soon to sort out all of this wretched mess; somehow she had to get rid of the spirit. There surely must be a way that Amidyne would know.

He could hear the phone ringing and ringing at the other end, until at last a female voice answered. It caught him unawares and nervously he blurted out, "You must come out to us and quickly."

The polite cool voice at the other end spoke crisply, "You do realise that it is a Sunday don't you?" Her voice then faltered, "I'll go and get my mother. It's her that you need to be speaking to not me."

Nervously James clung to the phone and within a minute a softer, calmer voice spoke to him. This voice he could relate to more, it was gentle and questioning.

It did not take him long to explain the position, and by the time he had finished speaking he could hear Catherine making preparations to get out of the bath. He listened intently to the soft voice at the other end.

"I cannot come during the week, though I can come this Saturday if that would be of any help to you. Would ten in the morning suit both of you?" In an equally calm voice James replied that it would be fine for both of them, and briefly gave details to Amidyne where to find them.

No sooner had he put the phone down than Catherine entered the room looking much calmer and relaxed.

"Who were you speaking too?" she queried.

"Come and sit down beside me and I'll tell you, it's something that you really want, and you're going to be so pleased about it, that I'll be in line for at least twenty brownie points." He grinned. "The clairvoyant is coming out this weekend to see us, so hopefully she will be able to throw some light on this whole spooky business and get rid of this wretched presence or whatever it is for good. In the meantime we will go and see Emma for a short while, that will take your mind off things for a bit, but for heaven's sake keep out of the study. Just don't go in there at all, I really mean that."

My whole being now relaxed. "That's great news, James, how wonderful," giving him a hug. "That has made me feel so much better knowing that she will be hopefully sorting it out soon. I'm just so pleased that I can't believe it."

James shrugged his shoulders. "It was a mere nothing madam, all part of the service, now have you got Emma's presents, if so we will be off, time is getting on?"

"Yes I have them already in my bag upstairs, though I don't seem to have got her anything exciting this time, I hope she likes them." With that she was off out of the room again, and bounding up the stairs. At last presents gathered together, a light lunch eaten, they locked the kitchen door, leaving Holly sleeping peacefully in her basket content to be home at last.

It was fun seeing Emma again. It made them both feel a lot more relaxed, as though things were back to normal for a while. "Where is my present then?" Emma was being outspoken as normal.

"You don't deserve one for asking," said James sternly, "where are your good manners girl?" he added jokingly. He could hear Catherine rooting about in her bag pretending that she had forgotten them.

Emma grabbed them with glee. "What's in them, mum, is it something nice?"

"Open them and see," smiled Catherine with the old twinkle back in her eyes again. "Open it carefully it's breakable so don't drop it, as I won't be going back to Cornwall again for a long while."

Curiously Emma opened the first present. Inside wrapped in mauve and pink tissue was an exquisite candle burner, which was more or less the same colour as the mauve and pink tissue paper. There were a few moments of silence. "It's beautiful," gasped Emma with delight, "was it made in Cornwall?"

"Of course it was, everything I bring back is made down there. Do you really like it, I know I did, I nearly kept it for myself."

"It's really lovely, mum, you could not have bought me anything better, I'll put it in the hall near the phone; then people will see it as they come in and ask where did you get that lovely candle burner from, then I'll say proudly, my mum. What is in this other one? Let me feel it first to see if I can guess what it is." Another few minutes were spent while Emma tried in vain to find out what it was.

"For goodness sake open it up and see," shouted James at last. "I cannot stand this suspense any longer."

Emma tore open the wrappings with glee. The back door then burst open with a bang making everyone jump in fright.

"It's only me," laughed Adam. "I thought you would all be here. Did you enjoy your hols, mum? It went very quickly to me; it only seems like a few days ago." Striding up to her, he bent his tall figure down to hug her. "I see that I have come at just the right time for present opening," he smiled mischievously. "I hope you have got me something, otherwise I'll sit and sulk for the rest of the afternoon."

Time passed quickly. It was good to be with them all again, like old times when they all used to live in Essex. What a long time ago it seemed now, like a past world and life.

The clock in the hall started to chime the hour, seven chimes, they had counted them one by one. "Time we made a move," sighed James, "it has been a lovely afternoon, but it's work in the morning for all of us, so we must bid you all a fond farewell and be away. The poor dog will be waiting to be fed and let out; she will be thinking we have deserted her."

Lots of hugs and kisses followed. It was good to be back, though I was still missing Cornwall, the cliffs and the sea. They felt as though they were part of me now, I missed it terribly. The drive home was quiet and subdued. I did not wish to return to the busy life of work, I was getting used to this easy way of life, and didn't want to go back into the rat race of jobs and work again.

That week sped by. It went far too quickly for me to even miss Cornwall again after that first Sunday. Whilst I had been away the computers had crashed at work, so that there were lots of input data to be put back on, which required attention and concentration, making me even forget the spirit and Amidyne coming at the weekend.

At last Friday evening came, when we were able to wind down at last. We opened a bottle of Cornish Mead and discussed what we would tell the clairvoyant.

That night I slept heavily and awoke very early to unknown footsteps walking across the floor, treading like heavy walking boots on a wooden floor – footsteps now in my bedroom, making a swishing sound as though walking through the room to the other side. I then heard noises on the stairs. Glancing at James's sleeping face lying beside me, I knew that the footsteps had been for my ears only. The presence was coming closer and into our bedroom that belonged to me, and James. My watch said it was five in the morning; James would not be stirring until at least seven.

All I wanted was to get out of bed and get on. I knew that sleep would not come to me now but my body was too scared to move. I was even too frightened to get up to go to the bathroom; it might be waiting for me outside the door. I knew it was silly but that is exactly how I felt. Every sensation in my body was tense. The presence was waiting for me to leave my bed and the protectiveness of James.

That next two hours went by so slowly, I tried to sleep but couldn't. I still felt so disturbed; in my imagination I kept hearing that swish of somebody going past me, and the heavy hollow footsteps on the floor. I don't think that I will ever forget it.

Those two hours eventually passed. I heard James stirring beside me. My mind was willing him to wake up, and to get out of bed so that I could follow and get up.

My mind wandered to the events, which would happen today, not long now until Amidyne came. I had hoped to be composed and ready for when she arrived, not a nervous tearful wreck as I felt now. Not wanting to make James anxious, I decided not to tell him about the footsteps that I had heard earlier. He had enough to think about.

James in the meantime had gone back to sleep. I sighed, luckily for me the phone started to ring. Who could that be, so early in the morning. I let it ring so that it would eventually wake James up, which it did, muttering curses as he staggered down the stairs, only to reach the bottom when it stopped.

"Blast and damnation," he grunted crossly to himself. "Who on earth is that at this time of the morning? I hope it's not Amidyne cancelling this morning." I heard him dialling a number, presumably to find out, who had rung. A few minutes' silence passed while I waited with baited breath. Was it the clairvoyant cancelling? Please, dear God, don't let it be that, she must come today, she must.

I heard James muttering again, "I don't recognise the number at all, and it is definitely not the clairvoyant's, so that's good it must have been a wrong number." He yelled up the stairs to me, "I'll make you a cup of coffee and bring it up to you in a few minutes if you like."

Familiar sounds from the kitchen floated up the stairs, making everything appear normal again for a while.

My anxious feeling suddenly going as quickly as it had come. I too clambered out of bed, and glanced at my watch, only a few hours now until Amidyne came. I really must get on now and quickly. Time was getting on.

This unknown lost spirit was indeed intent on making mischief between us and for whatever reason it wanted me to itself and nobody else.

James and I did not say much to each other that morning, each of us intent on what the clairvoyant was going to find out and say. Eventually after what seemed an age, the time of her arrival came. I was extremely subdued and James, I could see, kept twiddling his thumbs. He was very quiet, which was always a sign that he was really worried.

What would she say? Could she get rid of the evil spirit that was haunting us and this cottage? What was it that lurked in the study and prowled on the stairs, making our animals nervous as it did so? What made things open and shut? What made the television come on and the printer start up on its own? Would the clairvoyant be able to tell us. I very much doubted that it was possible for her to do so.

CHAPTER 6

THE CLAIRVOYANT

The doorbell rang shrilly making both of us nearly jump out of our skins.

I hastily jumped up in fright. James sat still and silent. I knew that he was going to leave all the talking to me.

I opened the door to a pleasant-looking woman. Her short-cropped hair looked clean and well kept, the round engraved earrings which she wore glistened and shone in the early morning sun. Her face looked slightly tanned with a scattering of freckles over it. She was someone who looked entirely normal. I suppose I had imagined a gypsy effect. It just shows how wrong you can be.

Amidyne seemed to have done this many times before. She was completely at ease with everything and us – someone who warmed to us immediately, talking to us for a while first of other spirit forms and presences on other planets, along with ones whom were lost on different planes and lanes like ours was. She told us tales of other people's ghosts. At least we were not the only ones with a problem, and by the time she had finished, we were more at ease. She gently started to question us on when had it all started to happen.

I was hesitant at first to explain, thinking perhaps that she would think us totally mad or deranged and just making it up. My worries were groundless. Amidyne was used to these happenings. She had seen and heard it all before.

I started talking slowly at first until gradually my confidence grew and I was talking about it all quite naturally. James was still very silent, as though not wanting to be part of any of it, as if he were ashamed of it all. Once more I felt a dividing gulf appearing between us.

Amidyne slowly and gently managed to make my words tumble out in a rush, every single thing that had happened. I spilled it all out in a long torrent of words. Sometimes my voice sounded shaky with emotion; a few tears crept in and caught me unawares. James remained silent his face frozen and still, making no attempt to help me along.

At last it was all over; everything that had to be told had been said. James at last made a move to make coffee; the wind had now picked up outside. We could hear it lashing at the windows and screaming down the chimney and the cottage felt sinister again.

Amidyne spoke softly, "I think it's time now I looked round your house on my own. It might take only one hour, or it could take all day. It all depends if the spirit is aggressive or not. It does sound as though it lives upstairs so I will concentrate on that part of the house first. Before I do that however, I do need to work on you Catherine for five minutes as I have to close your mind down to this form or spirit that is haunting you, as it has, I imagine, the power to link into your mind. It sounds rather frightening, but believe me it isn't at all.

"I just close your mind down so that it cannot harm you or enter into it so easily. Come and sit down on this easy chair. It won't take me long and I promise you that it will just make you safer; it definitely will not harm you at all."

I slowly and hesitantly sat down as I had been told, not wanting really to be part of any of it. My face felt pensive and worried, I was so nervous that if they could my teeth would have been chattering. What had we let ourselves into?

Amidyne was right, it did not take long. It had not hurt and when it was all over I felt slightly more relaxed and at peace.

I remained sleepily in the armchair, while Amidyne wandered upstairs quietly and alone. She had asked us not to disturb her, no matter how long it took. The telephone was to be taken off the hook, and no radio or television left on. She did not want any disturbance at all; her only wish was to be left entirely alone without noise until she gave us the all clear.

The rest of that day was endless. How on earth we got through it I just don't know, but somehow we did. How difficult it is to be quiet if you're trying so hard to be. We could even hear the clock ticking peacefully away on the wall amidst sudden outbreaks of the wind that was raging outside the windows. The rain had now started and that in turn was beating on the windows and doors. We heard the letter box rattling loudly. Was it the wind and rain, or was it due to something else much more powerful? Who knows, I certainly didn't.

Apart from whispering to each other occasionally and getting an attack of the giggles once, James and I kept quiet. I was feeling so much more at ease, but James looked as though he was hating every moment of it.

It was now two in the afternoon: three whole hours exactly since Amidyne had climbed those stairs. Was she alright? was she still alive? Had the spirit quietly done something to her without us knowing? At that precise moment we heard a terrific bang from above us in the study. We stayed very still, remembering what she had told us. Even if we had wanted to move, our legs were rooted to the ground. What had happened up there? Was Amidyne still alright? We hoped so.

It must have been a further ten minutes that we sat there, now very subdued and silent. A movement came from upstairs, then we heard her coming slowly and stiffly down the stairs shuffling as she did so.

White-faced she quietly came and sat down beside us, remaining silent for several minutes, as though all strength and words had gone completely from her. We also sat silently waiting for her to speak, trying to fathom out in our own minds what had happened up those stairs.

The clairvoyant, when she did speak, spoke so faintly that we could hardly hear her. "It has gone," she whispered, "but for how long I just do not know. What I do know is that eventually it will return. It has not gone for good, it has told me so." Amidyne looked as though she had had enough; all energy had drained from her. She was exhausted mentally and physically.

Eventually she spoke again. "It is an evil force that you have had here. I have done my best to reason with it to leave, and at least for now it has gone to rest on another plane. It will leave you in peace for a while but it will return again as I have already told you. It is not content, it loves you Catherine. It has told me so." With that she reached tiredly for her leather bag. "I must go home now and rest, for the time being I cannot do any more." Amidyne staggered as she rose from the chair.

James put out his hand to steady her. "But why is it here? What is its name?" I blurted out, Amidyne had come with peace in her heart, I could feel it and I did not want her to go.

Her reply was subdued. "It's an unhappy force that you have here. It was taken abruptly from this life and far too soon. It was not ready to go, and its name is George. You too Catherine have often been unhappy in your life, that is why it has attached itself to you, and only you. Somewhere there has to be a link to something between you both, though what it is I just do not know. My mind is too tired and I cannot think any more. I really am completely worn out; I must now go back to my own home to rest. It is time that I went."

James showed her to the door and opened it. The wind and rain had gone now and all was silent.

That evening it started to rain hard again and persistently; with no sign of the presence making itself known, the cottage felt empty and lifeless. Why we could not imagine, but we both felt it.

Several months of peace passed, though perhaps it is best that we cannot see into the future. I am still returning to the study to read, knowing that one day, and perhaps soon that the spirit will be back. The rain has gone now, but in its place is a warm high wind that moans and groans on its way round the cottage. I now go to bed to sleep with my husband James. I dare not sleep in the study any more, in case one day it returns and I'm there.

As each day passes we felt more relaxed, it was now late September nearly two years ago since I had the presence first visit me on that cold January night so long ago. I go more into the study now to read or write. Everything still appears normal like it should be. We sometimes wonder, James and I, if Amidyne, the clairvoyant, has laid everything to rest forever. Only time will tell, but everything for the moment appears and feels peaceful.

Possibly closing my mind down has also helped me, as I do not have the nightmares, which I once had. This has made me feel less tired and much more relaxed.

James is a quieter person now, not the old lovable James that I used to know. He has gone as if someone has put a barrier between us, or a hard lump of wood between us. For some unknown reason he is not the same man since the presence became known to us. Things I feel will never be quite the same again. Perhaps, who knows, James might need healing time. It could be that the presence did more damage than we had at first realised.

September what a beautiful month! It must be my favourite time of year. Blackberries have been picked, and the last few cooking apples are now off the trees. Some of them made into lovely tasting apple pies. The next thing will be hunting for sloes along the hedgerows on a misty morning or cool autumn evening, to make gorgeous sloe gin to hoard away in the cupboard for the cold winter yet to come.

As the cottage appears to be at peace for a while, we have anchored our roots down firmly once again at Broome Cottage much to Adam and Emma's delight. They adore it here so it pleased them very much.

The last two weeks have been lazy ones for me, the end of the holidays for the year. Two more days and they will all be over until the following year when we start all over again.

CHAPTER 7

SPIRIT CALLED GEORGE

As I relaxed lazily in my chair in the courtyard, I could see all the work in the garden that is yet to be done. Weeds seem to grow so vigorously when you leave them unattended even for a week. Our tiny lawn is in need of being cut again, it's all so time consuming and I shut my mind to it all. I start to relax then feel pleasantly sleepy and my mind starts to wander. I wonder who has lived here in this cottage before us. Was it a family, were they happy? I wonder why I have not thought of this before. It now seems terribly important that I find out more about who lived in this cottage before us.

James at that precise moment sauntered through the gate. What excellent timing I thought to myself. "It's a beautiful evening Catherine, did you hear those wild geese flying over," his eyes turned to me in a quizzical fashion. "Now what are you thinking about I know that look on your face, it spells trouble with a capital T." He ruffled my hair in a teasing fashion for fun. Anxious for James to hear my thoughts I blurted it all out in a rush.

"How can we find out who lived here before us in this cottage? Come on, James, you're supposed to be the clever one. Would any of the neighbours know, you must ask them?"

"What makes you want to know that all of a sudden? What does it matter who lived here; it's such a long time ago now. We must have lived at Broome Cottage for well over sixteen years now."

"I just need to know that's all, it's just entered my head. I just feel that there is a possible link somewhere; perhaps you could ask the old boy next door when you see him next in the garden. He has lived there for about thirty years, I'm sure he will have the answer."

It's really uncanny how things turn out. The very next day James was asked by our other neighbour if we wanted some tomatoes which Simon had grown. Eagerly we accepted. A head poked itself around the gate to look in our direction not wanting to miss anything. His wife Cynthia had come out to join us; she was a kindly friendly woman. I nudged James, my mouth moving to say, "Ask her, go on ask her now." I dug him in the ribs but harder this time, "Go on," I muttered again.

"Hi there Cynthia, we have just been admiring these lovely scented roses in our courtyard. Did the previous owners plant them here?" Cynthia smiled a knowing grin. We knew immediately that we were in for a fruitful piece of information.

"Alice that was her name, a lovely lady she was. It must have been years ago that she planted that rose bush, her husband really adored her.

"He made such a fuss of the roses after she died, it was so sad. They were such a happy couple and it all happened so suddenly. She was taken into hospital urgently one night, and that was that. Her husband was devastated. After her death he was so miserable we used to see his light on late at night in the study. He missed her a lot and used to stay up till the early hours of the morning making wooden toys for children. Nearly every night when we went to bed that light would still be on. Then of course he was found dead. The milkman had told us that his bottles were still on the doorstep. We told the police who then came and forced the door open. It was an awful shock; he had been dead for at least two days."

We heard Cynthia give a big sigh and for a few moments there was silence, her eyes met mine. "Where did they find him?" I heard myself saying, I felt James eyes on me as much to say, don't ask anything more.

"They found him in the cellar. Why he was down there of all places I just cannot imagine. It was a spooky old place at the best of times. He really loved every single bit of your old cottage and was so happy until he lost his wife; his life was really lonely after that, he missed his wife so much."

James spoke up at last, "What was his name Cynthia, do you remember after all this time?"

"Of course I remember he was called 'George', we used to call him old boy George." A dull silence followed, I knew full well that James was stunned as much as myself. George – of all the names that she could have said – George was the name of the spirit that the clairvoyant had mentioned. She had said a spirit called George haunted our cottage and was the cause of all our problems.

George had worked in our study late at night. The cellar where he had died was below it. Was that why it was always so deathly cold? Had he come back to this cottage hoping to find his long lost wife Alice? On what plane had she gone and why had they not met up together again? Had he died too quickly? Had his spirit remained behind to keep searching? What had Alice looked like? Did she resemble me, was that why the spirit George kept haunting me? Did he think I was his wife?

My head felt odd, as though I was now far away and I felt sick. Faintly I heard James thanking Simon for the tomatoes. I felt an arm guiding me back to the cottage – a firm hand pushing me down on the soft velvety cushions. "Are you alright Catherine, I felt as shocked as you when she mentioned the name George. It's just so unbelievable. That's who our ghost is, that's the name that our clairvoyant mentioned. I still can't believe it's George who died here in our cottage. It is the spirit of him who is haunting us."

The rest of the evening was spent going over it all churning it over, but still it was hard to believe.

George, who had loved his study, which was my study now, had loved his wife dearly. He had loved this cottage, and somewhere along the line it looked as though he loved me for he had come back to this cottage, but how and where this fitted in neither James nor I could fathom out.

What was the riddle or mystery to this thing that had been haunting our cottage? Neither of us knew the answer.

James looked tired. I felt depressed. Suppose all this new-found knowledge of George made the spirit of him return. Would he still haunt me like he did before? If it did return I resolved to move from this cottage. I could not and would not stand any more. I was beginning to dread and hate George and his wretched name.

We both cuddled up to each other that night for comfort, both of us in our own little world of thoughts. We were both scared of the unknown and of George.

It took us a long while to find the world of sleep, and when at last we did we woke up bleary eyed and tired. James stirred first. "Are you awake Catherine? I have been awake since early morning thinking. Let's forget we ever heard what we found out yesterday, or at least try too otherwise it's going to stir everything up all over again. We know now who has been haunting us, George. But hopefully it's now at rest and at peace. We must put this all behind us as a bad memory. We must be positive and look to the future." His words sounded as though he did not really believe that we could do that. Perhaps his thoughts were like mine that it would once again return.

After that day we did not speak of George again. We each in our own way pushed it all firmly to the back of our minds, hoping that it would never return to upset our lives again.

Several weeks passed without mishap. By now it was early in November, already all the shops were decked out with Christmas goodies and gifts. It was a time which Emma and I loved. Already she was buying presents and ringing me up to say that she had bought me yet another gift for Christmas. She was a tease, as she would never tell me what she had bought me only that I would love it. We started to make lists of what we were going to buy. I had made up my mind to buy special presents this Christmas, really nice ones all wrapped up in pretty gold tissue paper with red and gold bows. I probably said this most years though I was determined that this year I would do it.

A sudden bout of flu at work caused me to do long hours something I always hated. It was a nuisance as I was already tired and a bit strained.

Adam rushed in late one evening with his new girlfriend Carol. James liked her and so did I. She was such a happy-go-lucky person that you could not help but warm to her. Hopefully at long last Adam had found the girl of his dreams. We hoped so as we sometimes worried about him and it would be nice to see him settled down.

In view of Christmas getting near, James and I decided to redecorate the hall with new wallpaper and paint as it was beginning to look old and dingy. The decision was a bad move to make so close to the festive season.

It caused both our tempers to fly as it took such a lot of our precious time up. The old wallpaper was so difficult to peel off. James then upset the paint tin all over the hall carpet, which resulted in yet another visit to the shops to buy a new one, which really infuriated James and made him bad tempered for the remainder of that week.

It was now only four days to Christmas. The hall had only just been finished. I had somehow managed to buy all the presents that I needed, but alas no time to wrap them all up in the special tissue paper ribbons and bows, that I had wanted to do, that was far too time-consuming to do now. I made do with ordinary Christmas paper and string, not so nice but much faster, it got them all packed anyway. We did manage to go down to the woods to get a little holly and berries off the trees along with some mistletoe. Sadly we could not find the Christmas decorations. We spent a whole evening searching in all the cupboards and drawers, even in the loft looking frantically in every possible box that we could find, but they looked as though they were lost forever.

Once more tempers were well and truly frayed; even I was short tempered with Emma, which did not go down well with her at all.

The tears then started. I always cry when I'm tired or feeling down. Fortunately James knew me well enough to keep a low profile, while at the same time handing me a glass of wine. I have taught him well.

Regrettably I had to work Christmas Eve, so poor James ended up with all the shopping to do. He was far from amused even when I offered him fifty pounds to help towards it his face did not light up as it normally would. He took it in silence and walked away. I didn't have time to bear him a grudge; Emma, Adam and Carol would be over in the morning which would be Christmas Day. I just had to hope and pray that they would help matters improve. Possibly not, as by the time I arrived home from work with still all the preparations for dinner to be done that evening, I would be equally tired and bad tempered. At that moment I really resolved to have a far different Christmas next year. We would go away. Yes that would be the answer. I would snuggle up closely to James tonight and tell him – that might brighten things up.

On that thought I felt happier too. What did not get done tonight would just have to be left.

It was two in the morning by the time I finally climbed into bed. James was snoring loudly and I now felt restless and wide-awake. I slid out of bed again and walked into the study and sat there for a few minutes wondering about our spirit called

George. Would he appear at Christmas? I wondered and sat very still and silent for several minutes. I had thought he might come tonight as he seemed to be in my head for some reason. I waited for quite a while, but George did not appear. I heaved a big sigh of relief and softly tiptoed back to the warmth of James, the blissful bed and sleep.

After all the Christmas rush the next day went well. The family all arrived for once on time; presents were ripped open so quickly that I'm sure that no one noticed that there were no bows or ribbons on them. Everyone this year had remembered Holly; she must be one of the most contented dogs in this world. The day passed happily and so quickly until finally we shut the door at ten that night exhausted but content. It had been a good day; at last we could relax and unwind. We listened to the Christmas carols and fell asleep in our armchairs. The next day was Sunday then one more day and I would be back at work once again. Had it all been worth it? Not really, we wondered what the New Year would bring. The years pass by so swiftly now that I sometimes wonder where they go to.

No sooner was Christmas over than it was the New Year; Adam surprised us by getting engaged to Carol. They had only been together six weeks and simply adored each other. She was such fun to be with; secretly I was really pleased Adam could not have chosen anyone better. The wedding would be in late September which is my favourite month of the year. It would give me a little time to save up. Emma was delighted if a teeny bit jealous; she was the eldest of our children and still single. She was a fussy girl, but her time would come I was sure.

The New Year somehow seemed to open with once again a pessimistic note. Why I cannot even begin to explain though unknown to us there would be a further glimpse into the planes far beyond us. It was not only us that had ghosts.

It is now the middle of January, and winter is settling in with a vengeance. I have the long weekend ahead of me which is bliss. Still feeling sleepy from my long lay-in that morning I reach down to the wood basket to put some more wood on the blazing fire.

Faintly I could hear the postman bang on the door next to us. I then heard the squeak of our gate and his footsteps to herald a bundle of letters through our door, hopefully with a change from our usual pile of bills that come with endless monotony through the door. I hasten through the doorway to find quite a lot of mail on the mat which looks quite pleasing to my eyes.

A pretty coloured envelope stood out from the rest of the pile. It had been neatly written in black ink an unfamiliar handwriting, which I did not recognise at all with just the postmark Shropshire stamped on it.

I sat down in the armchair in comfort. James had already gone out so that I could take time to relax and read. Puzzled I tore it open in pleasurable suspense. Who could it be from I wondered? Strangely it was from a couple of friends whom we had not been in touch with for many years. They lived in this beautiful old farmhouse which was originally an old mill, deep down in the heart of Shropshire – a really desolate part of the country with no houses for miles and miles around. At one time they had been dear friends of ours, but work interferes with many things these days, and this was one of them.

Sue Ashcroft was inviting us down for the following weekend. Her husband John had been poorly recently. He was a lot older than his wife so that Sue was hoping we might be able to cheer him up a little, as he often still spoke about us. How exciting! It would be lovely to go down there and see them and the old farmhouse again. I promptly wrote and told them we would both be there on the specified date, not thinking to ask James first as I should have done.

Luck never had been on my side. The weather warning just before the date was really grim – bad gale force winds with snow and blizzards in places.

Should we postpone it I wondered as we pondered it over? James thought that we should cancel the weekend. I pouted. "I am really looking forward to seeing them James, come on let's still go the weather might change by then, let's be a bit adventurous for a change. It will be fun, for goodness sake don't be so stuffy James."

"Not if we get stuck in snowdrifts in the wilds of beyond in this weather," he muttered crossly collapsing on to the nearest armchair.

Persuasion at the highest level was now needed. I dropped down beside him. "Please James we have not seen them for years. It would be so lovely to visit them and the old farmhouse again we used to love it down there. Don't you remember the fun we had there, and John sounds so poorly we ought to go in case he ends up in hospital."

The minutes ticked slowly by, until at last he spoke. "When is it, next weekend? You may be right, the weather could change by then. Give them a ring tonight just to confirm everything then hope and pray that the weather changes before then."

"Is that a deal?" I heard my voice speaking with excitement. "The last time we went down there Holly fell in the lake outside John's farmhouse late one night do you remember that?"

He grinned. "How could I forget that one, I was the one that had to haul her out and dry her down. John's hall was like a river, she was so wet," a slow smile crossed his face, "and she stunk like a skunk, then on top of that she came and went fast asleep on our bed still wet, as you told me that she would catch her death of cold if we didn't. How possibly could I forget it?"

Time simply flew by the next week. James kept a keen eye on the weather forecast – each evening sitting glued to the television while I cooked our dinner. To both our dismay instead of getting better it got steadily worse. I feared that we would have to cancel it after all. Luckily James kept his thoughts to himself, for which I was grateful.

Funnily enough the Saturday we were due to set off the wind suddenly died down. It turned warmer and the snow started to melt. James was clearly relieved; he hated driving in bad weather conditions.

Eventually we arrived at our destination. The winds were still stormy but the roads thankfully were clear of ice, which was marvellous.

The farmhouse had not altered at all, and was still painted in a delicate shade of pink, with the stream running nearby. The front door opened as soon as we had parked the car as though they had been watching for us. Both John and Sue had aged considerably. I suppose they possibly thought likewise. John now had to have the aid of a walking stick and a part-time nurse to help him. He always had been an independent gentleman so this all made him very irritable and short tempered. The farmhouse was just as we remembered it. As you entered the front door, there was a long concrete floor in front of you, a dining room on the left, and a very posh sitting room to the right; the continuation of the hall led you to a wooden floored clad office, as old fashioned as you could imagine. Beyond this were the stairs to the six bedrooms above; in the middle of the upper hallway stood another set of stairs to which we nicknamed the Gods, consisting of a massive room. At one end was a huge old fireplace which they lit in the colder winter months. There were numerous settees of all shapes and sizes all covered with beautiful coloured throws. At the opposite end stood a massive oak table which groaned at the weight of food which was piled high at celebrations and Christmas. Beyond that the original shute of the old flour mill stood, as a beacon of many centuries ago when bread was real bread. This huge room was classed as the boardroom for when they held large meetings. John was now an ex-member of Parliament so those days were far gone, though the room was still used many times for visitors as it was so impressive. John clearly loved this room it was his utopia where he spent a lot of his time writing his diary. When you looked out of the windows you could see for miles around. A moat surrounded the farmhouse so that when you woke up in the mornings you would spy a kingfisher or heron swooping down upon the water, and an otter if you were lucky or early enough to catch a glimpse of one.

I myself longed for a few days' holiday there. It was so enchanting and old fashioned that it was like stepping back in time. My chance came sooner than I expected at the evening dinner that night.

The meal had been as always superb. Maggie, the housekeeper, who had been there twenty years, had as usual excelled herself in providing a perfect and unusual meal. It was over a glass of wine that the opportunity arose.

The conversation had been mainly between John and James while Sue and I were content to listen. John was so interesting, despite his age and ill health. He was a witty and intelligent man still, who kept us all enthralled. John also loved to show off; if he had an audience he would keep them all up until the early hours of the morning. The stories would keep flowing and everybody would be amused and enthralled. How we all loved it and what a change it made from our humble abode at home.

Amidst the conversation we heard the door opening. "May I clear the table away Mr Ashcroft, have you all finished?" I had been so engrossed that I had not heard Maggie softly walk in.

"Of course you may my dear, then you must be away home it is getting rather late. Is it in the morning that you travel to your daughter's or am I getting mixed up with next weekend? You know how easily confused I get these days."

"It's in the morning Mr Ashcroft that I go. Victoria has her operation on the Monday morning so I must try to be there for when she starts to recover, especially as her husband is away abroad. I will be away for a least a week." Maggie's face looked worried. "Will you be able to manage without my being here?" She glanced at her employer's expression in a questioning fashion.

"We will have to manage without you somehow my dear Maggie. How I don't quite know but one thing you must not do is worry, you will have your hands full with Victoria so you must not even think of us."

Sue looked worriedly across the room at me, her eyes then went downwards to her plate. "There is no doubt that you will be sadly missed, but I expect that somehow John will manage without us both." Sue then looked again at me. "Just to double the trouble I have promised to go away with my brother on Monday for a week in Scotland. He will be so disappointed if I don't go, and besides that he has paid the full booking fee of the cottage. They don't come cheaply nowadays it would be a shame to waste it and I know for sure that he would not go on his own. John says he is quite capable of staying by himself here at the farm but I wonder whether I should get a nurse in to help him."

Her conversation was short-lived. "Don't you even think of such a thing," her husband's eyes blazed with sudden anger. "I don't want any strange nurses or such like roaming around our farmhouse snooping and poking, I can well manage on my own." Still looking very annoyed he blew his nose loudly, which indeed ended the conversation.

Sue looked anxious and her frown deepened, without hesitation or thought, I heard myself blurting out:

"I can take some of my holiday if you would like me to help out with the cooking and looking after John. It would make a lovely change for me. You both know how I love this old farmhouse and I would be company for John." Out of the corner of my eye I could see the amazement on my husband's face, as if to say she's lost it, lost the plot completely. Shaking his head he turned back to his plate and was silent.

John's face was a different story: it showed unconcealed delight and pleasure. Sue broke the silence first. "That's simply marvellous," she shouted, "when can you start?" Even Maggie was pleased and suggested that, before we went, she would do a sort of hand-over procedure. Arrangements were made for me to start on the Tuesday, which left only one day to give notice of my holiday at work. They too would not be pleased at such short notice.

James was quiet, not seeming at all pleased with my offer of help at Watermill Farm, but I was thrilled to bits. A gorgeous whole week to roam in this beautiful farmhouse all on my own with only John for company.

The drive home was in silence. James was angry, really angry.

"What on earth did you go and do that for?" He spoke quietly, a sure sign that I had indeed annoyed him. My lips tightened.

"I just don't know what all the fuss is about, I'm only staying there for six days. I'll be back home Sunday night. You know how I love that old farmhouse. It will be lovely staying there, just think of me for a change and not yourself for once." The rest of the journey was in silence. The next day Sunday I packed and James kept well out of my way, making sure that I was asleep before he too came to bed.

I left early that Tuesday morning glad to get away from James and his black moods.

CHAPTER 8

THE LADY OF THE NIGHT

With excitement I arrived at the farmhouse as promised. John was really pleased to see me though I could see that he was not at all well that morning, so I relaxed and made a light luncheon for both of us. I knew he loved egg sandwiches made with brown bread and butter so that was an easy one to start with. While the eggs were boiling I gazed out of the kitchen window. What a wonderful view it had from all windows. It would have been paradise to live here forever, what bliss! After lunch John just wanted to sleep. I found some books to read, time now for me to unwind for a little while.

That evening John was still not well, I kept wondering whether I should call the doctor or not. He insisted that he sat in his favourite armchair in the television room, and no he did not want to go to bed so once again I quietly withdrew, wishing now that I was back at home. Perhaps James had been right, I should not have come here. I amused myself for the rest of the evening by sitting in his office flicking through his enormous book shelf – books of every kind you could find – a bit like an Aladdin's cave. I was soon in another world. Books were part of my life; I loved them so much. I was soon lost in them forgetting where I was and all of my troubles for a while at least. It was late by the time I roused myself and glancing at my watch, it was time I checked on John, then took myself off to bed. It had been an odd sort of day, not the sort I had expected.

Feeling concerned I peeped in the television room before retiring myself. He was still there just where I had left him last, staring into space looking past me directly to the staircase. It was as though he was not seeing me, but through me.

I could hear him faintly muttering, so leaning more closely to him, his tone dropped to barely a whisper though I could just hear the words 'the white lady', before he finally succumbed to sleep. My mind was buzzing. Who was the white lady? I resolved that when John was his normal self again I would ask him who the white lady was. Perhaps they had a ghost here too. Perhaps every house had a spirit of some sort. I felt cold with a sense of foreboding. Had something followed me here, I wondered – possibly in some form of different spirit? Had it been sent to shadow me, to follow my every movement? A further bout of shivering enveloped me. It felt cold as if something was very close to me or to John.

I gently put his feet up on the foot stool and covered him up with a warm blanket, hoping that he would still be with us in the morning. Softly I crept towards the door closing the door quietly behind me, I heard him gently give a deep sigh.

My legs wearily climbed the stairs to bed. Hesitating on the staircase I looked up. Fleetingly out of the corner of my eye, I caught a brief glimpse of a white figure at the top of the stairs. The white lady. Could it have been her? It had all happened so quickly and unexpectedly, and in a flash it was gone, or had it been my imagination? How could I tell, how could I find out? I would just have to be patient and wait.

As I crept into my cosy, old-fashioned comfortable bed that night, I wondered how old the farmhouse was. All I knew was that it had been a mill many centuries ago. It had the feeling of character, as though shadows were hiding within the walls waiting to show themselves at any moment. It felt creepy, or was that due to the long corridors and steep staircases? It felt as though it had a story to tell and was waiting for the right moment to spring out. At long last I fell into a fitful sleep waking up every hour for no apparent reason at all.

I awoke in the morning to the sound of the postman's van chugging its way down the long drive. The bedside clock had its hands on nine in the morning. I had overslept which was most unlike me and on my first morning at work too. I would be in disgrace. Throwing off my bed covers I hoped that John would still be in his armchair, or else in bed asleep.

Hastily I dressed dragging on any old clothes in sight. Would John still be alive? How awful if he had died in the night under my care. Horrors I must not think like that. Without a thought of putting my make-up on or cleaning my teeth I tore down the long staircase to John's little study where I had left him asleep the night before.

The study door was as I had left it. I pushed it half open with the toe of my foot and peeped round. There was John as I had left him though this time gently snoring. An overwhelming feeling of relief flooded my whole being. What on earth had made me think that he had died?

Wearily I walked towards the kitchen; a strong cup of coffee was what I needed and now.

The following couple of days I got to know John really well. He would tell me story after story about the old farmhouse with humour, knowledge and love. I learnt that the farm originally dated back long ago to the year 1200. In that time it was purely and simply just a mill for flour making. The mill had then been gradually added to bit by bit, an extra room here then another one until it was the huge one as it stood today. Families had lived here for generation after generation. I questioned him about ghosts and who the white lady was; Johns face immediately became a stiff mask. He said there were no ghosts or a white lady. The matter was firmly closed. Therefore the matter was not referred to again.

John was extremely slow in walking, so my heart sank when he suggested we go into the nearest market town to buy a film for his camera.

Much to my surprise the afternoon turned out to be most unexpectedly pleasant. I had managed to drive his jeep without landing in a ditch, though I did smile at John's agitation at my driving skills. If I exceeded thirty miles per hour John would say 'slow down you're going much too fast in this jeep.' He was certainly from a vastly different era to the one which we both lived in now.

In all we had a most pleasant if slow afternoon. We eventually drove back in the warm hazy afternoon sun. Life was good at the moment and I did not seem to have a care in the world.

That evening I made the dinner extra early. John and I were both exhausted from our afternoon out. John was slow eating his dinner that night which was annoying. In the end tired of waiting up, I bid him goodnight and left him in his little dining room which he clearly loved so much. I awoke the next morning to blustery skies. John had somehow dragged himself up to bed on his own, probably in the early hours of the morning. I left him there until he called for me. By that time it was midday which meant that the afternoon would be boring and slow.

After his breakfast I spent a lot of time with him up in the vast room upstairs or up in the gods as I called it. He wanted time looking through all his old photos of years gone by when he had been in the First World War. This took ages and for me was tedious and slow. I kept glancing at my watch, until the daylight slowly started to fade and grow dim. It was always at this time that I got these sinister feelings as though shadows of the past were drawing nearer and closer to me, as though the spirits of the past were calling out to me. John carried on. He lived in a world of his own and sometimes he was oblivious to myself or anyone else around him.

Vaguely I heard the wind rising. On the news it had said that gale force winds were once again on the way. Being practically minded I asked John where the candles were kept. He shook his head vaguely. We spent the next couple of hours looking for them. On our hunt we found things that John had long forgotten about until at last we discovered a few candles tucked away at the back of a cupboard, about seven in all not enough really but better than nothing. Certainly not enough for a large farmhouse like this if we should happen to be cut off from electricity. I called to John to stop searching for any more. It was wasting so much of my time. Three of them consisted of long red tapered chandelier ones. I put these in the appropriate holders in the hall, the rest in the dining room and the last two in the kitchen. Luckily both of the torches worked well, they were the rather large old-fashioned ones that seemed to always keep going and going for ever.

In view of the weather warnings I decided to cook dinner early that evening in case the gales got worse and turned the power off.

The wind outside had risen even more to gale force. The windows started rattling as though an old man was shaking them. The radio started crackling and another feeling of unease crept over me as the lights started to flicker on and off. How thankful I was that I had managed to find a few candles and matches, plus the torches.

Hastily I put the dinner on: bacon, eggs, fried bread, sausages, and mushrooms. An odd dinner but it would be quickly done and hopefully while there was light and power. Luck was with me for a while until I had cooked John's meal anyway. It smelt good and made me feel hungry. John looked pleased as I put it before him. His appetite was always good; if I had served him a plate of fried worms I'm sure he would still have eaten them. He was game for anything. I had only just left him safely with his dinner in the dining room when suddenly we were pitched into total blackness. I panicked and headed to where I thought I had left the torch. It wasn't there. I was certain that I had left it on the table in the kitchen. My hands groping frantically for the torch or even a candle, nothing. I stood still for a few moments trying to calm my pounding heart. They just could not vanish into thin air. Where were they? Once again I took firm deep breaths. They had been on the table I remembered putting them there. Slowly I turned my body round to feel once again on the kitchen table. My hand straight away felt the solid torch. Mysteriously they were now back on the table. Torches and candles were in the same position as I had left them though they had certainly not been there a few minutes earlier.

The room felt creepy as though something had happened here long ago, perhaps centuries even. My scalp prickled. There was a presence in the room. It felt sinister. Was it George following me or was this another form of being which should have gone on to another plane? Swiftly I lit the candles. Once they were burning I felt better. I put two in the kitchen, two in the dining room with John and the three red tapered ones in a special holder together on the hall table. I checked that the front door was locked and bolted then drew the heavy velvet curtains across. I could hear the wind lashing to and fro outside. Surely there would be some trees down in this hurricane.

"Catherine are you there?" I heard John shouting my name.

"I'm coming." Quietly I checked the front door again. I was extremely nervous tonight. Was something going to happen, would it be to do with the white lady? Who was the white lady?

My mind already growing weary, my footsteps walked slowly into the direction of the dining room and John.

The hall felt cold. I entered the dining room shutting the door firmly behind me as I went and sat opposite my old friend.

"That was a delicious meal, my dear, and this candlelight is so pleasant we must light them more often. Is there a dessert to follow I wonder?"

"Yes there is John I'll just get it for you." The kitchen felt its normal self again. I relaxed and went to the fridge to reach for his bowl of stewed apples and pot of cream to go with it. Swiftly taking it into him, I remembered that I had not given him any wine; turning towards the door to enter the hall I noticed that the door stood open a little. I had definitely shut it. I knew I had. Another feeling of coldness touched me, boldly I went towards the door. "I'm just going to get some wine John, I won't be a minute." Choosing a bottle of red wine I gathered up two glasses and, shutting the dining room door once again with a definite resounding click, I poured out the wine for both of us. We were on our fourth sip of this most delicious wine when I felt a cold draught on my neck. Spinning round to the hall door I could see that it was slowly opening to reveal a space just large enough for a human being to pass through. I shivered, my scalp tingling.

Without a word to John I tiptoed into the hall. There was no sign of anything or anyone. There were no windows open, the velvet curtain was still firmly across the front door and yet I could still feel this icy cold draught coming from some unknown source. I stood there alone for several minutes. To my left there was the long flight of stairs, and to my right the front door, which held the thick heavy velvet curtain where no possible draught could ever penetrate. My eyes then rested on the candleholder, which had held the three tapered red candles. My body tensed and froze. The three red candles had gone, disappeared completely. My body felt rigid and freezing cold. I crept up to the candleholder and forced myself to look at where they had been. I shuddered again, no sign even of any burnt candle wax it was as though someone had taken them swiftly and silently away. I stood still and looked towards the dining room door yet again just in time to see it slowly and silently opening, knowing that I had firmly shut it behind me again as I had crept out.

A feeling of utter panic descended over me. The hall was strangely quiet as though I was in a time void of many years ago. I couldn't even hear the wind. Diving now for the dining room door and the safety of John's presence, I stumbled in and sat down. It was warm in here and cosy. I could hear the wind again outside howling away and as forceful as ever.

"Are you alright my dear, you look a bit shaky? Do please have some more wine." John pushed my glass nearer to me. Picking it up I must have gulped it down in two mouthfuls.

"I just feel a bit tired John that's all. It's getting late. I'll clear up then perhaps get along to my bed." Perhaps I'm imagining things I thought to myself, glancing towards the door again. It had now opened once more. I felt panic rising once again. I just wanted to get out of here. It felt strange. "Can you feel a draught John and have you noticed that the dining room door keeps opening?" I saw John glance towards the door.

"The door is closed Catherine," looking at me oddly he pointed, "is that the door that you are talking about?"

"Yes it is, you must think I'm imagining things but it won't stay closed."

"It is shut now, my dear, and I am positive that it has been shut all along. Why don't you pop to bed, perhaps you're over-tired."

I knew that he was trying to humour me, so I quietly said good night and went into the kitchen to make myself a nightcap. Sleep. How could I sleep after that experience? I would be too frightened to go up the stairs even, for a while anyway; I knew what I would do. Have my nightcap and get on with some writing.

It was cosy in the kitchen now, my bag and bits and pieces were laid out on the kitchen table as though nothing had happened this evening. The wind was dying down to a faint whisper and the power had just come on.

Leaving the candles to burn themselves out I sat thankfully down to my letter writing. I did not get far. My eyes were feeling sleepy. The longing for my bed and sleep overcame me so quickly. Putting my pen neatly down on the table my eyes turned to the clock ticking merrily away in the corner, my bleary eyes told me that it would soon be ten thirty. Yes time for bed – for once I would have an early night. It would be nice to snuggle deep down into the duvet covers and forget about John. He would get himself to bed eventually.

Sleep, sleep – that's what I desperately needed. Slowly I eased myself out of the chair, my legs stumbling over the edge of a torn carpet, my hands immediately shooting out to save myself. A searing pain shot up my arm as I struggled to gain my balance. Quietly standing there for a few moments until I did so, a feeling of great tiredness creeping over me once again. What was the matter with me? Determinedly I staggered towards the staircase and bed.

I do not even remember climbing the stairs or even undressing. Sleep must have overcome me almost immediately, for whatever reason I do not know.

That night I had a really strange dream. I dreamt that I was back at home and sitting in the dining room. The evening light was failing quickly and turning to dusk, when suddenly our two French doors flew open with a tremendous crash. Startled I scrambled hastily up from my chair to shut them immediately. They burst open again with such terrific force that it made me gasp. Whatever was happening I made a third attempt to shut them again, but another force of wind came yet again. I could hear myself screaming out for help trying at the same time to hold the doors from swinging open again. In the far distance I heard the faint sound of running footsteps and shouting. James and Adam appeared from another room, "What on earth is going on here?" James yelled at the top of his voice striding quickly to my aid. He too could feel the force of the wind. With both his and Adam's hands they held the French doors shut. "Turn the key for goodness sake will you," he mouthed the words as a deafening noise filled the room. I turned the key viciously in the lock. Slowly, to our amazement, the doors very slowly started to swing open once more bringing with it a deathly and eerie silence.

I then awoke yelling and screaming. I screamed and screamed until it suddenly dawned on me that it had been a terrible nightmare. It had all seemed so real, so frightening as though it had really happened.

Thankfully I turned over to put the bedside lamp on. Glancing at my alarm clock, I saw that it had only just turned midnight. Still feeling ill at ease, I felt as though someone was searching for me. Who I wondered? Could it be the spirit of George? The name George was speaking in my head. Surely not George, not here, not within this beautiful remote farmhouse.

My stomach churned. I had no one to protect me here, no one at all. I was virtually on my own. John would be of no use at all if the force came to get me. What did it want, was it here with me now or was it purely a figment of my imagination? I found myself perspiring, beads of moisture had broken out on my forehead and were trickling down the sides of my cheeks; I started again to shiver violently and could not stop.

Ring James, yes that was the answer. I would ask him if he would come over straight away to spend the rest of the night with me. If he jumped in the car right away it would only take him an hour to get to Watermill Farm.

I breathed in great gulps of air. I needed lots of courage to get myself into the hall and down the long flight of stairs to the telephone below. Did I have the strength to make it? I was so terribly scared. Saying a silent prayer I made a beeline for the door, grasping the door handle with sticky fingers I wrenched it wide open. Peering nervously around the door I looked out onto an empty hall. It felt empty but I knew that it wasn't. I could feel eyes upon me from the far corner that was the oldest part of the mill that dated back to the thirteenth century. Without a further thought I dashed down the stairway to the telephone below.

Frantically I dialled the number at home. The phone rang and rang, my hands clenching the receiver tightly. I let it go on ringing for ages. I was just about to put it down when somebody at the other end picked it up.

"Hello, hello James is that you?" I was sobbing loudly. I could hear the phone airwaves on the line, somebody was there but not answering. I listened intently, feeling slightly calmer I spoke again. "Are you there James, please answer me?" My ears could still hear the airwaves though more faintly this time. I then heard a quiet click as the phone went immediately dead.

My hands held the phone piece for what appeared a very long time. Slowly I put it down. Who had been there? Somebody had picked it up but who? I was so puzzled that for the moment I had forgotten my fear that something was here in this farmhouse with me.

Somebody was at home with my James and it was in human form. Perhaps a woman how was I to know. We had not left on good terms and James had not seemed himself for quite a while now.

The name George spoke again inside my head. My body turned immediately icy cold. I was beginning to know these signs. Something, which was in spirit form, was deciding to pay me a visit. A faint movement in the far corner caught my eye and the room was beginning to get even colder. My body tensed waiting for whatever was going to happen next. The lamp by the side of me flickered; something light and feathery touched my cheek. Hastily, I spun my head round, to see rising from the chair in the hall a figure of a lady covered in a long pure white velvety gown. She was smiling at me as though she knew who I was. My body felt as though it had turned to stone.

I opened my mouth to scream but as I did so the white figure started to disappear, then she was gone. My body felt physically sick. She had been so close to me. If only I had been able to touch her with my hand, would she have then spoken to me? Who was the white lady and would I ever know?

What I needed desperately now was a hot drink or else something a good deal stronger. Could I gather enough courage to enter the kitchen? The answer was no. I turned tail and ran swiftly up the stairs back to my bedroom and the safety of bed. Why oh why had I not bought my dog Holly with me in the car.

I would not be feeling so irrational if she had been here with me. I snuggled deep down into the bed pulling the covers over me as far as possible. Eventually after what appeared hours I fell into a deep exhausted sleep.

I awoke early to the sound of the telephone ringing. Hastily pulling on my dressing gown I stumbled down the steep stairs yet again and into the hall. My hand reached out when it immediately stopped. In the faint distance I could hear John's mumbling voice, it must have been a call for him. Disappointedly I turned away, deep down I suppose I had been hoping for a call from James. We had not spoken to each other since we had the argument about me coming to stay at Watermill Farm.

Was he getting fed up with the situation? I wondered. It was not his thing to be mixed up with ghosts and spirits. He was far too practically minded to believe in such things, but he must now be very much aware of their existence.

I heard myself sigh. Oh well I had decided earlier on that I was not going to be the first one to ring, let James do it for a change. He was the one with the problem. Angrily I swished back the heavy velvet curtains in the hallway. The hall, which had looked so sinister last night, appeared friendly and normal, the sun filtering through the tiny window at the side. Had it been my imagination, or was I on the brink of a nervous breakdown or were there really spirits shadowing my every move.

Shaking my head in bewilderment, I opened the front door, the wind had dropped, and the air smelt damp with a faint hint of fog hanging around. In the distance I could hear the crows and jackdaws making a noise, and in the shrubs nearby a frantic twittering was going on.

I wondered if any trees had fallen in the gale last night; perhaps after lunch I would take myself off for a walk while John had his afternoon nap.

That same morning quite a lot of mail had arrived for John which enabled me to have a little more time to myself in the kitchen. No sooner had I made myself some coffee and toast, when I heard a car come speeding down the drive. It pulled up behind a clump of tall bushes. Keeping a close eye on it, I wondered who it could be.

Within a few minutes a youngish lad came into view holding what looked like various gardening tools in his hand. My mind immediately clicked to the gardener called Richard. That was who he was. I remembered John telling me he came three days a week, this must be one of them.

Swiftly I put the kettle on again and rushed out before I missed him. At the top of my voice I called out, "Richard would you like some coffee?" He halted what he was doing and spun round with a puzzled look on his face. "Hi I'm called Catherine. I'm looking after John this week while Sue and Maggie are away."

His face broke into a smile. "That would make a nice change at this time of the morning." My hand reached out to shake his. It felt steady and firm. My first instincts told me that I could trust this young man like my own son. Possibly he might know who the white lady was.

Richard was friendly and appeared pleased to be sitting in the kitchen chatting. I relaxed and talked to him about the garden and asked him where else he worked. Richard lowered his voice then raised his eyes to the ceiling above. "You have to be careful what you say. John always says to everyone that he is deaf in one ear, but he isn't. He hears what he wants to hear, so just be careful what you say," a smile flitted across his face, "he can be a crafty old devil at times."

My look of surprise must have shown visibly. "Don't get me wrong he is a marvellous old boy, but he certainly is not deaf like he says he is."

This opening up of confidences gave me the lead that I had hoped for.

"This farmhouse is so old; surely it must have a ghost in a farmhouse of this size. It's hundreds of years old. Have you seen any Richard, it has a feel of having some especially at night when it's dark?"

It was silent for a few minutes while Richard gazed out of the kitchen window sipping at his coffee whilst deep in thought. "Funny that you should say that," lowering his voice once again he spoke eagerly and quickly. "John says there isn't any ghost and always gets most annoyed if people even ask about one but there must be several. I for definite know that there is one lurking about as I have seen it." This was just what I had been hoping for.

"What have you seen Richard and where? Did it frighten you, come on tell me?"

"If I tell you too much you won't want to stay here at night as it will scare you." I knew that he was teasing me.

"What did you see, please tell me, there is something isn't there. I really feel that there is a presence of some sort in the farmhouse. I felt it last night."

Richard helped himself to another biscuit then looked at me to study my face. "Are you quite sure you won't be scared if I tell you what I have seen like ghosts, clomping old boots, and things that go bump in the night," he grinned and settled himself more comfortably in the chair.

"Things like that don't scare me." I was lying dreadfully and hoped that it did not show in my face.

"Okay if you're sure. It was quite a while ago now; in fact it must have been last winter when the evenings get dark early. I was round the back walking past John's office about six one evening, the lamp was on and it looked kind of cosy. I couldn't see anyone in there so I decided just to quickly have a peep in through the window. As you know John's office is long and narrow with a flight of stairs leading to the side of it and the opposite side a long corridor. Whatever it was I saw a movement near the door at the end of the room. It just simply glided along the walls as though it was floating in the air – the movement was so gentle it just seemed to glide. It was only for a few brief seconds. I was petrified as though I was in that same room with it before me, as if I was in another world with this tall white lady shrouded in a haze of white. Honestly I was so scared that I didn't have time to study it. I just ran straight back to my car and went home."

There was silence Richard now looked visibly shaken as though he was being cast back in time to that very evening.

Several minutes ticked by before he continued. "To tell the truth it just scared me so much that now I don't hang around. When it gets dark I just go home."

"Can you tell me in more detail what it was like?" I questioned him carefully. "You must have remembered something else about it surely?"

"Honestly if I knew more I would tell you Catherine, though I did have a feeling that it belonged there, and it was definitely in pure white, and it glided as though on ice. It was a ghost I was certain of that and not a figment of my imagination." Richard was now looking quite shaky and pale as though he could picture every single detail in his mind.

"Have you spoken of this to anyone else?" I asked gently.

"I told my girl friend when I got home, she laughed at me, and I think I told Maggie the housekeeper here, she didn't seem at all concerned. She just said that probably the farmhouse was full of ghosts from the past, and things like that did not worry her."

"Have you seen anything else?" I asked, "recently I mean anything since the white figure that you saw that night?"

Richard shook his head vaguely. "No I haven't. That was the last time that I have been here after dark, and I rarely come into the house now, as John has not been too well of late. He always makes sure that Maggie gives me my wages." His eyes glanced towards the clock, immediately he swung his legs off the chair. "I must be off now Catherine, thanks for the coffee, just don't mention to anyone what I have said about the ghost, not even to Maggie. Promise?" His eyes looked anxiously into mine.

"Of course I won't. I promise I won't breathe a word to anyone and I mean that Richard I really do."

It was strangely quiet after he had gone. John was evidently still busy with his mail, otherwise he would have called down to me by now wanting help with his bath.

Churches, why had churches suddenly sprung to my mind? The church in the village – I was somehow convinced that something there would give me a vital clue as to whom the white lady was. Not having been round the graveyard in the village, the thought had not even entered my head. Churches and graves were not usually my type of thing. I turned the possibility slowly over in my mind; it might somehow be interesting to visit it. Possibly it would certainly give me an insight as to who had lived and died in this rather quaint English village.

I vaguely remembered seeing the church as I passed through the other day with John. From memory it lay back beyond the brief scattering of shops just outside the village. It was backing onto fields and looked a very peaceful spot. I resolved to give John an early lunch the next day. That would give me a chance to explore a little on my own in the afternoon. Hopefully, John would be content to doze in the chair after lunch like he usually did.

Breaking into my train of thoughts the phone started to ring in the hall. I just let it ring thinking that John would pick it up but he didn't. Feeling irritable, I crashed my cup onto the kitchen table and flew to answer it.

"Mum is that you?" I recognised immediately that sunny happy voice.

"Emma!" I shouted with delight. "What a wonderful surprise, how come you're ringing at this time, it's Wednesday you're usually at work now?"

I heard a giggle in the background, "I should be, but I kept on thinking of you down there in that lovely old farmhouse so I told my boss that I needed a few days' rest. I was getting burnt out as the saying goes, so he told me to take the rest of the week off. Isn't that great mum? I can come down and see you. Would it be okay if I came for a few days?" She paused while I thought for a moment.

There was a silent delighted pause on my part. I could not believe my luck. I was to have this fun-loving daughter of mine to stay for a few days with me. At that moment I would have given her the world if I could have done so, I was so pleased that I would not have to spend another night alone in this farmhouse.

"How simply wonderful Emma. How quickly can you get here? John will love the extra company. How long can you stay? It's been a little eerie here all on my own, and John has become so deaf that he isn't now the intelligent person that he used to be. I'm sure that he would not even hear an army coming through the door, bless him."

Without giving time to give poor Emma a chance to reply, I rushed on in full flow. "I'm just so pleased to know that you're coming to stay for a few days. Have you spoken to your father lately?" The words came out in a rush, and my heart suddenly seemed to be pounding much faster as I spoke those last few words.

What would Emma say in reply? I could sense her hesitating as though she was at a loss as to what to say next. "I did ring him last night mum, but he wasn't in."

"What time did you ring him Emma?" another pause

"Sometime in the evening I suppose. Why do you ask?" she now questioned.

Emma never could lie. I knew she had rung him late that evening, something was telling me so. "Was it after ten last night because I phoned him much later after that and he wasn't answering it."

Dubiously I heard Emma saying, "Yes, I thought he might be feeling a little lonely without you there mum, so I just thought I would give him a quick ring to see if everything was okay. As you say he was out though goodness knows where he was at that time of night. It's not like dad not to be at home, anyway what time can I come over?" Impatient as ever Emma now just wanted to be on her way.

"Come over as soon as you can. I'll expect you some time this afternoon, drive carefully."

"Bye mum, see you soon." The line was silent; all thoughts of churches and graveyards were chased from my head. What fun to have Emma for a few days and what a lovely relief, for I was beginning to dread the nights in this old farmhouse, something was going to happen and soon.

John! I suddenly remembered John. I must give him the good news; perhaps some young blood about the place would brighten him up and possibly make his brain sharper and more keen.

Blast the phone was ringing yet again. Then silence. John must have picked it up promptly for once. Quietly I moved into the hallway to see if I could hear who it was. I turned the handle to open the inner door to hear more clearly, but something appeared to be tugging at it. I tried to open it again, and felt it slowly open a fraction just enough for me to feel a cold fresh draught touch my face. The door then mysteriously opened just in time for me to see the front door curtains moving and the keys in the lock swinging to and fro.

My body froze. Something was still here with me. I was now certain of it, as with sinking heart I turned towards the stairs and John. The stairs looked dark and dim as though the sun had gone in, something was still lurking and waiting. Did it want me out of here? What exactly did these unknown spirits want of me? I felt so glad that Emma was now on her way. The spirits might then possibly leave me alone for a while at least.

I entered John's room with a smile. He was pleased to hear that Emma would be arriving shortly and demanded his dinner more or less immediately. He did so love having visitors and it gave him a new lease of life every time someone visited.

By the time John had eaten all of his lunch the clock was steadily ticking on. Would I have time to cook a batch of scones before Emma arrived I wondered. Perhaps I would risk it. Hastily I washed all the dinner things up first then concentrated on my baking. I spent the next couple of hours or so in the kitchen. The scones had risen up beautifully, some with raisins and sultanas and the rest with dates. They had only been out of the oven for half an hour when I heard the doorknocker go. "That must be Emma!" I shouted. Without waiting for a reply from John, I ran to open it, wrenching the door open. There stood my daughter looking so excited at these unexpected few days off.

"Hello mum, I'm here at last. Are you okay?" giving me a hug as she flung the words out and eyeing me shrewdly as she did so. "What's the matter mum, you're looking ever so peaky?"

a look of concern flashing across her face. "Has it been too much looking after John? How much longer have you got before Maggie returns?"

I felt my lip tremble a little at those kind words. "Not long now Emma. The worst is over, only a few more days then hopefully I'll be back home again," my mind flashing back to James and what he had been up too.

"John has been much more tiring than what I thought he would be. In a way it's been rather a strain, and I have missed Holly far more than what I thought I would. It has been lonely here and the house is very spooky at night. I'm sure it's haunted."

"Haunted!" shouted Emma in delight, "you must tell me more."

CHAPTER 9

JAMES

The car drove swiftly and quietly through the large white gates
and ground to a halt. James slammed the car door shut with an
almighty crash. Catherine, he was so fed up with her. Why had
she suddenly got it into her head to stay with John of all people?
He just could not fathom out. All he wanted now was a normal
life which simply meant some fun and laughter, having someone
warm to cuddle up to at night, not someone who was in tune
with ghosties most of the time.

Catherine had changed. He had changed, the house had
changed. It was perhaps time to find pastures new and soon.

He could hear his footsteps crunching noisily up the gravel
path leading towards the kitchen door. James stopped. The house
looked cold and empty, his eyes resting on the study window he
thought for a moment that he saw a movement behind the
curtains. Holly was barking away inside the house. She had
evidently heard his arrival, or was she barking at something else,
which was inside the cottage.

James felt at that moment that he did not want to go into the empty cottage alone. What other choice had he but to go in? He must go in even if only to let the dog out. Perhaps even just to pack his case and go, but to where there seemed nowhere to go and why should he, nothing could hurt him in there surely.

This cottage, which at one time he had loved so much, appeared now so sinister and evil.

James felt his neck start to tighten, beads of perspiration started to gather on his forehead and trickle slowly down his face. Reaching down to his pocket his hand shakily pulled out a handkerchief, anxiously mopping his face his eyes turned once again to the empty study window. No movement at all, nothing. Surely it was all in his imagination? Holly was barking even more frantically now making his mind and limbs jump into action. He had to go in. There was work waiting for him, a pile of mail waiting, and a dog wanting to be fed and walked. Still he stood there willing himself to go in. His ears could now hear the telephone ringing inside the cottage. Could it be Catherine he wondered, phoning to see if he had arrived home safely from work, or to see if Holly was alright? Probably the latter knowing the way they had left each other.

With one more quick glance at the study window, James gathered his keys and work from the car and went purposely towards the kitchen door. There certainly was no more time to think with Holly dancing about for food, cuddles and walks all in that order preferably in that sequence.

James then realised that the telephone had stopped ringing. It would surely ring again if it were anything important it usually did.

Despite Holly getting extremely excited with the attention of James arriving home, to him the cottage felt empty cold and lonely. Once Holly had been sorted out, James looked in the cupboards for some sort of dinner for himself. A brief meal of a variety of tinned food would have to be sufficient for his stomach. His eyes looked at Catherine's dog stretched out and asleep on the hearth rug. If only his life was as simple as that at the moment. Tomorrow night, my girl, I am going to drop you off at Adam's for the evening as I'm going to treat myself to a Pub meal for a change.

That night James turned the lights out early so he did not see the shadow that was once again waiting quietly on the stairs, or the owl that hooted softly in the nearby oak tree, James was already asleep.

The alarm clock at last roused him from a deep dreamless sleep. "Blast I should have got up earlier. I have Holly to do yet. I had forgotten about her," muttering sleepily to himself he staggered tiredly towards the bathroom.

Frantically he showered himself, leaving no time for thought he was off.

Eventually, once more back at work, he wondered how on earth he had managed to do everything without being late. Holly had insisted on going for a run, jumping up and down in excitement leaving hairs all over the suit that he was wearing, until at last James had got the magic lead out and taken her for a run. Returning to the cottage he had bundled her straight into the car. His aim was to take her round to Adam's in his lunch break and leave her there until things were more sorted out in his mind. Adam loved having her so that was no problem. It was he himself, James, who needed to have time to think. What was he going to do? No way was he going to return to Broome Cottage that evening to be on his own. Last night had been fine. Somehow he had slept well with no intrusions from anything or anyone, the big question was would he be so lucky tonight? His own mind had made the decision already. Catherine would not be back home until the weekend. She was quite safe there. It was quiet on the work front at the moment, only a few courses that he was booked on which could easily be cancelled at the last moment. Holiday time – what had he left? That was the problem. He doubted whether he had got much at all. Slowly flicking through the calendar on his desk he roughly guessed that he might possibly have about a week left. That being so James reached for the phone to speak to the head of the University where he had lectured for the last ten years. The line was picked up instantly. "Charles is that you," James was speaking quickly, feeling all of a sudden rather nervous at this on the spur of the moment request; it was not like him at all. "Charles I need some time off urgently, as a matter of fact as from tomorrow Wednesday. Don't ask me why it's kind of personal. I just need to get away for a while. Can you get a locum to stand in for me until the end of the week? I will be back on Monday that's for definite."

"No problem at all James," the voice sounded concerned. Can I be of any help at all, you only have to say you know that don't you?" By the tone of Charles's voice James could tell that he was puzzled by this sudden leave of absence. How could he say that he, a grown man, was too frightened to go home to an empty house as his wife was away?

"I just need some time off. I have things to sort out which need my immediate attention," James's firm tone of voice reassured his boss for the moment anyway.

"Alright James I will arrange cover for you as from the morning. Take care I'll see you Monday." The conversation was then ended. James held onto the receiver for several minutes still not at all certain that he had done the right thing. What on earth was he thinking of? Where was he going to go? What would Adam think to all of this, and would his son be able to have Holly at such short notice and for the rest of the week, that would be the next question?

"Yes Adam I was going to drop the dog off at yours in my lunch break, but if you're not there I'll drop her off tonight about five or just after. I have all of her gear in the car. I'm sure I have not forgotten anything and she will love being with you. She must get lonely at the cottage without your mum about. I thought I might drive overnight down to the West Country. I just need a little break away that's all. I must go now I have a class to do in a few minutes, see you later Adam and thanks." Before Adam could refuse James had hung up, leaving his son hanging onto the phone in disbelief that he had so easily agreed to have Holly.

James turned away from his desk; a slight grin appeared on his face as he gazed quickly out of the window. It was windy and dull outside not really the weather to going touring down to Cornwall; the deed was done now so no turning back. His eyes turned fleetingly to the old fashioned clock on the wall. All he had to do now was finish his last class of the day, drop Holly off, then go quickly to the cottage to pack a small suitcase and be away. With a sigh of satisfaction he grabbed his specs and books then made his way briskly to his last lecture of the afternoon. It went well. His pupils had been attentive and willing to listen and learn. They too seemed to want to leave on time which certainly made a change from the usual questions that he received at the end of a class.

At last it was time for him to leave. James looked in his wallet; a visit to the hole in the wall might be wise before he went any further. It was only just around the corner from the University, that was the last thing he wanted was to be short of money.

The wind was now picking up, at least that would keep off the rain that had been forecast for today. Buttoning his jacket up, he strode purposely out of the building and towards his car.

After a short distance James pulled into his son's drive, noting that the kitchen light was on. Adam was already opening the back door to let him in. "Hi Dad, time for a drink before you go?"

"Sorry but no, I still have the journey back to the cottage yet, and I have not had any time to pack my case or to find my map so I really must get on, but thanks anyway."

Holly had already disappeared into the kitchen, thankful to be somewhere that she knew and loved. Adam always made a great fuss of her. He now threw her ball at her, as though suddenly unsure what next to say to his dad. Something was up that he was sure of, but what. He would ring his sister tonight; see if she knew what it was all about.

James feeling uneasy just wanted now to get away.

"I will see you in a few days Adam, thanks for taking care of the dog. With determined strides he headed once more for his car, then with a single wave he was pulling out of the gate and onto the main road which would lead him to Broome Cottage.

Time was already getting on. Should he stay the night in his own home or would it be best to drive solidly through the night to the West Country?

James could feel a headache coming on. Was it tension or tiredness creeping in? Perhaps a start in the early morning would be best after all. Sleep surely would be best, blow the spirit of George away. Why did it always have to haunt them and make one afraid, surely it would not appear without Catherine? His mind at last made up, he turned off the ignition key and headed towards his front door.

Things looked normal to him, or at least for the moment it felt cosy and warm like it used to be. He now wished that he had kept Holly with him. His intentions had somewhat back-fired. He had not reckoned on staying the night here. Oh well, he would be off at first light and it would be easier without the dog.

Once inside the kitchen he opened the fridge door to peer inside – sausages bacon, eggs, tomatoes, bread to fry – yes a good fry up meal would surely make him feel better in more ways than one. Carelessly he flung his jacket onto the chair nearby and started to prepare himself to be head cook and dish washer for the night, not hearing the wind rising to a gale outside and oblivious to the creaking of the stairs. James turned the radio up louder and opened a bottle of red wine, his favourite. Time now to relax and unwind and to make the most of a couple of days rest, away from the cottage. At daybreak in the morning he would be gone. It would be great to be going away for a few days to read and unwind.

A faint noise startled him. It sounded like a gentle clanking sound. The piece of fried bread that he had been holding fell silently to the floor.

The sound came from somewhere near the cellar door which was at the far end of the kitchen. His eyes looked up to see the pair of scissors that hung on a hook above the door swinging to and fro as though a strong draught from somewhere was moving them, or as if someone had brushed past them. His whole body stiffened, his second sense telling him that something was about and it was not in human form either. Slowly he finished his meal, his ears listening intently for any strange or new sound. Nothing, nothing at all, it was deathly quiet. He could feel his body relax a little and his mind settled once again on Catherine.

James could feel the pressure easing away from him. His supper was tasty and good, the wine pleasant to his palette relaxing him even more. He realised suddenly that the telephone had not rung even once. Catherine was indeed giving him the cold shoulder. Making up his mind to ring her, he walked from the kitchen into the hallway. Without warning the light bulb in the hall shot completely out of its socket immediately striking the wooden flooring and smashing into hundreds of tiny little pieces. He cursed softly. Feeling slightly alarmed, he looked up at the empty socket. His thoughts were chasing each other around in his head. He had never seen that happen before, must have been a power surge or something of that sort. Blast it I'm certainly not going to ring my wife in the dark. Feeling somehow subdued, James headed for the stairs and bed. He had taken far too long over his meal. His suitcase still had to be packed, a bath to be had, also where was his map and where had he left it last? It was several years since he alone had visited Cornwall. He would surely get lost if he did not have one. Realising that time indeed was getting on, two at a time he mounted the stairs.

Whilst running the bath he dragged his suitcase from the spare room, quickly he gathered his basic needs for the journey, it would then only leave the map to find. After a hasty bath

James put on his old comfortable bathrobe; his thoughts had returned to the map again. When had he last had it? Possibly it could be in the dining room drawer downstairs. Blast and blast again, his inner self was saying, don't go down those stairs again not until morning. He knew deep down he was frightened, really scared, but he must find the map. There would be no time in the rush to get away early in the morning to find it.

He could feel the solid wood beneath his fingers holding tightly onto the banister railings. The bureau in the old dining room downstairs – that was where it was. He was positive now that it was in that room somewhere. Turning back to the bedroom to grab his glasses, he descended down the stairs into the gloom below, through the hallway where the bulb was missing and into the dining room. His hand found the light switch almost immediately and he felt his heart lift a little when the light flooded the room.

So engrossed was he searching the drawers one by one for the precious map, his eyes intent only on one source, that he did not see the dark shadow hovering just inside the door, or feel the sudden coldness and stillness penetrate the room. It wasn't until he heard a movement up in the room above that made him aware that he was not alone any more.

He could feel his body freeze and grow rigid. The coldness was intense now. His ears picked up the footsteps again in the room above. The coldness started to recede but the footsteps were now in his bedroom above this very ceiling that he was now in – the bedroom that he usually slept with Catherine. Oh God what should he do? The keys to his car, everything, was upstairs in that room. He could hear the phone ringing and ringing in the hall but James felt powerless to reach it. His feet turned to stone; his ears listened intently for any further movement or sound. He felt as though the phone had been lifted off the receiver and something was listening intently, only to replace it a minute later which heralded the phone ringing once again. Ringing and ringing it went on and on, until suddenly it stopped. All was deathly silent for the moment.

James turned his body and faced the door. He could see the light flickering in the kitchen, a shadow of little twinkling lights in the corner of the window that started to dance across, as his eyes stared at them, showing utter darkness beyond.

The room was definitely getting warmer. He could feel the warmth once again creeping slowly back through his body. The movement upstairs was louder, he could hear the floorboards creaking again, then utter silence like a grave.

It appeared an age that James stood all alone in that dining room, until at last summoning all of his courage he timidly climbed the stairs to his bedroom. Slowly he turned the door handle of his room. He knew that he had left it open; something in the meantime had shut it. Every muscle in his body was twitching with nerves. He pushed hard at the door until it started to swing gently open with a slight groan.

"Give me courage please give me courage," James whispered to himself. Unsteadily and nervously he slowly entered the room. The sound of the telephone reached up to his ears again only for the phantom ghost to answer it like before. James crept round the corner of the door to see beyond and into the room. There before him on the bed lay the map that he had been searching for. It was torn up into tiny pieces.

James felt his mouth turn dry. His eyes crossed to the chair beside his bed. He caught a quick glimpse of a movement. This movement turned into a tall black figure which then stood up appearing as if from nowhere.

Dragging on his clothes, then grabbing his suitcase and keys, James lunged for the door down the stairs and out into the night air beyond. Sweating profusely he started the car up, sweeping out of the drive at top speed but seeing a motionless figure watching him from the top, landing window.

That night was long and lonely; James just drove and drove not seeing the road or the houses beyond. How he arrived in the West Country he did not know. Those hours in the night had become lost forever. All he could remember were those last few terrifying hours at Broome Cottage. Never again would he stay there alone.

He did not stop until he was actually inside the boundaries of Cornwall. Clad in a warm padded jacket, James climbed out and stood for a moment to breathe in the sharp early morning air, a feeling of freedom coming with it. His eyes took in expanses of fields and gentle brown-coloured slopes, slate grey small cottages nestled in the folds of the hills and mist clung in the valleys. A robin in the branches of an elder tree sang a note before dipping over the hedge and out of sight.

James stood for some time looking over the fields and valley lost and deep in thought.

The golden glow behind the clouds brightened and the sun's warmth began to penetrate the early morning mist. James went back to his car and settled himself comfortably in his seat, a feeling of peace with him at last.

The hotel car park was nearly empty as he drew up. He needed to be with people. Catherine and he had stayed a few times at this hotel on the coast and it bought back pleasant happy memories. He would spend the next few days planning what he was going to do with his life. Sadly he knew that eventually it would be without Catherine. The spirit was too much for him. He would leave it to his wife. It was her spirit after all and not his.

When Catherine returned home he would also return but not before and then only for a while.

The hotel was welcoming and warm, looking much the same as it had done many years before. He would stay in the hotel until the weekend. If Catherine had not returned home by then he would stay with Adam until she did.

As he left the car warm drops of rain were beginning to fall, splashing on the rocks and dotting the gleaming surface of the water. Far out to sea a fork of lightning stabbed across the darkening sky and thunder rolled in the distance. Without warning the rain fell in vertical sheets of sleet. James raced across the pathway to the hotel, which stood as a haven to him at that moment in time. Once inside he felt a strange sense of belonging, a crazy desire to accept this unexpected new life. After all what was there now to keep him with his wife? They were steadily drifting further and further apart with this evil spirit weaving in and out amongst them. James's life had been a quiet one, his work unexciting, somewhat like his marriage. Now it seemed life might take a bit more exciting turn. His trip to Cornwall had been quite impulsive. What if he should decide to move to Cornwall? Would it be with or without Catherine? In these next few days he knew that he must make his decision, the die was cast and he knew it.

Shaking his wet coat out, James headed towards the reception desk.

The young girl at the desk gave him a polite smile. "Room fourteen is free, Sir. It has a good view of the moors and it's nice and warm. The weather seems to be getting chillier now. Have you stayed here before?"

It was his turn now to smile. "Yes though it was many years ago, I stayed here with my wife and two children. I must admit the hotel does not seem to have changed too much." He thankfully took the keys of his room and headed off towards the stairs and room number fourteen. The bedroom was indeed cosy and warm, just as the receptionist had said it would be. Glancing at his watch he was amazed to see that it was already approaching mid-day; his stomach gave him a warning grumble. James suddenly realised that he had not eaten anything since his supper at Broome Cottage the previous night. Hastily emptying his weekend bag, he hurried into the bathroom to take a quick shower.

Feeling refreshed he sauntered down the stairs for a brief lunch, deciding quickly on beef sandwiches and a glass of beer. That would be quite sufficient until the evening meal. To his astonishment it took him at least an hour to demolish his light lunch. His body now felt better and was telling him that what he needed was some good fresh air in his lungs and some exercise to throw away all the cobwebs. He felt alive now, all he wanted to do was to explore this forgotten territory. It brought back memories of good times and laughter. With this happy thought in his head James strode purposely out; he already had a warm jumper on, along with his stout leather walking boots. As he wandered towards the door, the sound of laughter floated from the direction of the bar which was stationed a little further on. He saw a smartly dressed woman in green and for a brief moment their eyes met and held. James glanced quickly away, his mind already on other matters. It had been several years since he had last been down here to the Cornish coast with his wife. His mind vaguely remembered a lovely cliff walk not too far from where he was staying. A good walk would dispel all negative thoughts which were now tumbling into his mind. James strode out deep in thought onto the track, which would lead him to the coast path.

So immersed in thought had he been, that James had not noticed that the fog was rolling in from the sea. The sun had completely disappeared and darkening grey clouds were now obliterating the familiar landmarks.

James knew a moment of anxiety. He stood quite still and listened. If he could hear the sea then at least he could keep well away from the edge of the cliff. He strained his ears, but was unable to hear any noise, the fog now clothing him in moisture had the effect of deadening all sound. James pushed down a tendency to panic. He tried to remember where he had been walking. If it was the path that led to the beach, the sea and cliffs would be on his left, but which now was his left? The fog by now was so thick that he felt utterly disorientated and afraid to go either forward or back. Hesitantly he took a few steps in what he hoped was the right direction. He stepped into a hole, stumbled and fell onto his knees amongst some gorse bushes, crying out in pain as his hands plunged into the spines and prickles.

Silence followed, the sea mist flowed over and around him chilling his every bone. James shouted out but his voice sounded muffled and distant. He peered about him straining to see if some form of landmark was visible. The silence that followed was eerie but not threatening in any form. He was alone on the cliffs, utterly alone, but he did not feel frightened like he had been those few nights back at Broome Cottage. He breathed a sigh of relief. There was no spirit here to haunt him, it had already returned to Catherine. It had no business with him now that they were apart.

Safe in that knowledge he looked more keenly around. Something appeared suddenly out of the fog beside him. He stiffened, then realised that it was a collie dog from a neighbouring farm. The dog wagged its tail and hurried on. At that precise moment the heavy mist cleared slightly enabling his eyes to see a tiny bit further to his left, a sigh of relief escaped from his lips. He was well away from the cliff edge and now could recognise with difficulty his way back. Thankfully he slowly followed the cliff path back to his hotel and safety, for the next few days at least he could relax and enjoy himself.

That evening after finishing an excellent meal he made his way to the bar wondering if would see the lady in green that he had first seen at lunch time. Her face for some reason held in his mind. She had looked nice, calm, happy and intelligent, all in one. After scanning the bar briefly for a few minutes he turned away disappointed. Perhaps she had already gone home, perhaps even with her husband. Surely someone of that calibre would be spoken for. With that final thought in his mind he took to the stairs and bed. After sleeping for at least ten hours, he awoke to the sound of rain on the windows. Wretched weather, what a good job he had some decent books to read, which he had hastily thrown into his suitcase.

It turned out to be a pleasant day after all; the rain had eased off by about early afternoon so once again he turned towards the cliffs for exercise and peace. The wind had turned to the northeast; it was now decidedly fresh in fact quite chilly and damp. Perhaps after all he ought to return for his jacket. Swiftly turning back he swung rather impatiently through the hotel's swing doors. Hearing a swift cry of pain, he turned swiftly to find that he had caught someone's heel of a shoe in the doors. "I'm so sorry I do apologise, I could not have been looking where I was going." He looked round to see the lady that he had sighted on his first day. "My name is James Wood, please let me buy you a drink or were you just off somewhere?" She looked startled for a moment and clearly did not know what to reply. Somewhat embarrassed, he found himself saying, "I don't usually ask women for a drink but it's the least I can do after jamming your shoe in the swing door."

"Well I suppose that would be very nice thank you." Her voice was soft with a slight lilt to it, the smile lit up the whole of her face. James thought what a pleasant one it was. The next hour flew by; afterwards when he was alone again he could not even remember what they had spoken about. All he knew was that they had exchanged names and telephone numbers, that was all, but he had liked her, yes he had liked her a lot. Her name was unusual – 'Felicity Coates'. He had not known a Felicity before. Storing her name carefully into his wallet, he proceeded towards his evening meal and bed.

James took the journey back home on the Sunday; he had heard from Adam that Catherine would be back home on that day. His face was grim, as he drove his car away from Cornwall. Driving along he felt that the autumn had made its presence known with a more determined ferocity. The gales roared in from the west bringing more heavy rain. The trees bowed beneath the weight and the last plums and apples were shaken from the boughs. The pain inside James made it impossible for him to feel happy at returning to Broome Cottage. His decision had now been made; it had been made that day on the cliffs when lost in the swirling fog. The decision had been made firmly – no time to look back. Within the next month he would have to tell Catherine and his beloved family that he would be leaving to somehow start a new life in Cornwall.

The spirit had won. James would never compete against it again; to even try to do so would be madness. The spirit wanted Catherine alone and it would make certain that it did so. Thoughts were travelling through his mind at top speed. He resolved that he would not tell his wife the sad news at first. Let it wait a few days until she had settled in then announce his time bomb. It would be heartbreaking but it had to be done. He now had no further choice in the matter. If he James stayed at the cottage the spirit would do untold mischief, even kill him if necessary, for it appeared to have the power to do so. A cold shiver went through his body; yes he had now put up with this long enough. It was now time to depart though the thought filled him with dread. His love for Catherine would never die.

CHAPTER 10

MILL HOUSE

The look on Emma's face was a picture. She imagined that Watermill Farm was full of ghosts and spooks. No way on earth would she ever fathom out that all of this was connected somehow to me and my past life which scanned back possibly through centuries and beyond. How and when I would tell Emma was anyone's guess. I, as her mother, longed to let her know everything that had happened here at the farmhouse and at home, but I knew deep down that the timing had to be right otherwise Emma would just laugh and mock me. Things were simply and purely black and white to her. It was as simple as that.

"Haunted whatever do you mean mother?" Emma was suddenly dancing up and down with excitement. "Do you really mean haunted and in what text? What have you seen, what is it? Oh do tell me mum, was it at night-time? Have you told dad, will I see it, is it spooky, oh come on tell me?"

Emma's face was happy. Things suddenly appeared brighter and clearer now that my daughter was here with me.

"Calm down Emma, for goodness sake be sensible for a few minutes at least. I'm probably just a bit stressed out and imagining things. You know what I'm like. Look John is so looking forward to seeing you. If you don't go and talk to him soon he will get annoyed and start ringing his bell."

Emma, with a look of annoyance, picked up her bag and slung it carelessly on her shoulder.

"I had better show you to your room first. It is on the second floor next to mine. It's a bit shabby but the view over the lake is out of this world. If you're lucky you might see a kingfisher or heron early in the morning. You never know, or even an otter. I have not seen one yet John is the only one who has."

"It sounds lovely, I'm so glad I have come down." Impulsively she gave me a huge hug. "Come on then Mother show me to my boudoir at once this very minute."

I led her into the long stone clad floored hall and up the steep flight of stairs to the bedrooms above. Reaching the top Emma touched the carved wooden banister with delight and stood still. "Mum did you realise that these banisters are really loose, look they are really unsafe." With one hand she rocked them. "If anyone should trip and catch hold of it to save themselves from falling they would be down the stairs like a shot, especially if John is unsteady on his legs like you say." Her look was of instant disapproval as though I should have discovered that for myself.

"You're quite right, they are dangerous. I'll have a word with John probably his maintenance man will come out to secure them in the morning." Emma was already forging ahead along the long narrow hall looking out of all the windows with excitement like a young child, and poking her head through every bedroom door that she passed. "What magnificent views, mum, you can see for miles and miles. How lovely to stay here when it's snowing. Which is my room?" she added. Flinging her bag on the floor a puzzled look crossed her face. "It's quite basic isn't it, I thought going by the rest of the farmhouse it would be fabulously furnished." Emma's keen eyes took in the faded curtains which were riddled with holes, clean but very moth-eaten. An old ancient writing desk stood in the far corner nearest to the window. An equally old dressing table which held two candleholders and a tallish full-length mirror. The bed stood against the far wall nearest to the door. This was covered in a creamy coloured old-fashioned bedspread which must have been at least thirty years old. Before I could reply a voice bellowed loudly up the stairs making us both jump in surprise.

"Is anyone up there, Catherine has your Emma arrived yet?" Silence followed he was evidently awaiting an answer knowing full well that we were up there.

"Come on," I whispered. "I'll introduce you to John. He is inclined to be deaf in one ear though Richard his gardener says it is all put on."

I heard Emma give a giggle beside me. "Are you up there?" John's voice penetrated again.

Hearing a slight hint of annoyance in his tone, rushing to the top of the stairs I called out at the top of my voice, "Yes John we are both up here. I'm just showing my daughter to her room, then we will come straight down."

"Don't be long, my dear," his voice now holding a note of authority, which I had not heard before, "I am in need of some of my marvellous herbal tea."

I glanced round to Emma who had disappeared completely. A head poked out from behind the next flight of stairs which led to the massive boardroom at the very top of the farmhouse, her face beaming with delight. "It's super up there mum, just out of this world – everything is so old and the views are all simply stunning, has dad ever seen up there?"

"Come on daughter, I'll have to put you on a lead. John wants his tea and to meet you, he gets so impatient nowadays he is completely spoilt and pampered."

"Okay I'll soon sort him out." Giving me a mischievous grin she raced down the stairs ahead of me. "Which room is he in? There are so many doors. Where do they all lead to I wonder. I suppose you know where they all go to don't you mum."

Firmly I placed my hand on her arm. "Just follow me Emma, I am now going to introduce you to John, then after that we will explore the house and gardens together. That is if you can get away from him he does talk rather a lot."

"Shall I ask John about the ghost?" retorted Emma suddenly. Immediately my steps halted.

"Don't you dare mention anything of the sort to him, haunted houses or ghosts he will not talk about for some unknown reason. It just makes him irritable and he does not like hearing about that sort of talk." Firmly I opened the dining room door to be greeted by John's beaming face looking towards us. "This is my daughter Emma." John held her extended hand for a few minutes.

"I am so pleased to meet you, my dear, you look a pretty young thing. It will be pleasant to have some young company about the house for a change."

"I'll make us some tea while you have a chat with Emma." Without waiting for a reply I headed towards the kitchen to make a little light tea for everyone. Reaching for the freshly baked fruit cake that I had made I realised that I had completely forgotten to mention the wobbly staircase to John. That I must do at the next available conversation that I had with him.

The meal that evening was great fun. Two bottles of wine had been opened and John was in his glory telling us story after story making Emma reel out with peals of laughter. It was getting late by the time everything had been cleared away. I gave Emma a gentle push, she looked weary. "You go along to your room now and get yourself to bed, I have to see to John yet. If you're okay I'll see you in the morning,"

"But I have not seen the house yet, or the story concerning it being haunted." Her lips pouted which was a habit that she did frequently if she could not get her own way."

"There is another day tomorrow, now off to bed and I'll see you in the morning. My room is right next door to you if you should need me."

We gave each other a hug and kiss, then I returned to my chores and John. I too was tired but reluctantly still had work to do.

That night everything was peaceful and we all slept well though things were soon to change, regrettably for the worse.

The following morning my daughter was up early, eager for me to show her the farmhouse. "Hurry up mum, let's look round before John wakes up, you did promise." Emma was watching me curiously and she smiled quickly.

"For goodness' sake don't be so impatient. You must have inherited that streak off your dad. It's certainly not in my genes thank goodness. Before I show you round the farmhouse I need a good cup of coffee inside me and as you're already up you can do the honours please by making it. By the way have you got the time on you as I think perhaps I have overslept a little this morning. By the time you have made coffee I'll be down. Do you remember where the kitchen is?" She nodded. "Alright I'll see you downstairs shortly." The door closed firmly behind her.

I kept my promise I knew better than to keep my daughter waiting and I desperately needed my cup of coffee.

By mid-morning Emma had explored every nook and cranny around the house. I had been surging ahead with things so that I would have some time with her that afternoon and had left her to her own devices.

Vaguely I heard the phone ringing. "Can you please answer that for me Emma. If it is for John he is still in the bathroom getting dressed, he should not be long now."

It seemed an age that she was on the phone. What was keeping her on it for so long? I wondered, puzzled and now suddenly curious I went through the hall to investigate, but Emma replaced the receiver just as I entered the room. She stood for a moment lost in thought, then shook her head, folded her arms across her chest, changed her mind and stuck them in her pocket.

There was an air of anxiety and uncertainty about her whole demeanour which made me stop in my tracks. It had already been a demanding and exhausting few days and I did not want any more problems. Emma spoke quickly with a fraught note in her voice; sighing heavily I sat down in the hall chair and listened with growing concern.

"It's dad," she hesitated, "that was Adam ringing to say that dad has dropped Holly off at his for a few days while he has a little holiday down in the West Country." I stared at her in disbelief. "He did what? When did he leave the dog with Adam?"

"I think he said Wednesday night." Emma was looking even more worried than before.

"Surely that was the night I tried to ring your dad, he didn't answer it but I'm sure that someone picked it up. I'm certain they did, someone else was with him I know there was?" Suddenly there was a hint of tears in Emma's eyes.

"Are you saying that he was with someone there that night, a woman perhaps is that what you are thinking?" Loyal as ever to her dad Emma had spoken with fire in her voice. Wearily I rubbed my forehead, and then laid my hand on the velvety cushion by my side.

"I really don't know what to think anymore. Your dad and I have had a few problems over the last few months, I don't know what is going on. He is tired, I'm tired. It's not really making a good relationship between us."

"What isn't making a good relationship between you both, just what is the problem between you?" Emma looked me straight in the eye as she spoke. I could feel a headache coming on. A voice inside me was telling me to let Emma know the whole story, but how could I, Emma would be so frightened, or on the other hand she might not believe me and laugh at the whole thing. No way would she be convinced that what had been happening was true at Broome Cottage.

Emma's voice broke into my thoughts. "Cheer up mum for heaven's sake, when dad comes home next week and you're back as well, you will see it all in perspective. You have taken on far too much here at the farmhouse. Surely you would have been better off at home with dad?"

A door banged upstairs and the floorboards started to creak and groan; I gazed up towards the stairs. "That will be John I expect, he will be needing my help soon." Wearily I stood up. "I just don't know why your dad has taken himself off to Cornwall without ringing me first, it isn't in your dad's character to have sudden impulses like that. I don't like it at all, I really feel that something is wrong."

Emma pursed her lips and turned away.

I smiled ruefully at myself and tried to pull myself together. "I'll go and see to John now," and quietly left the room.

John that day was extremely slow and tiresome continually wanting attention either from myself or Emma. "I came down to see you mum, at this rate I might just as well have kept at work and left you to it." She moodily turned to the window and stared out to the garden beyond. I watched her, whilst my own mind was already in a different world.

It would be such a relief to have something to plan, something to take my mind off my unhappiness with James and the frightening visits by the spirit at the cottage, turning my mind resolutely away from my husband enjoying himself in the West Country without me.

It could possibly be that in the end they would have to sell Broome Cottage. I would hate to leave it but it looked as though the sacrifice was a necessary one, and it would be good to see James happy again.

There had not been one word from him since his departure at Adam's. I hoped that he was alright. My mind went over and over the terror, and loneliness since all these weird things had started to happen.

"Penny for your thoughts." Emma's voice suddenly breaking into the silence, made me jump hence bringing me back to reality with a jolt.

"I was just saying to you, mum, do you think Adam will marry Carol? I really like her, she is so much fun."

I smiled. "Yes I like her too, she always appears to be happy. They seem to be a perfect match but it is early days yet. They have not been together all that long, though I have not seen Adam so happy for years. Being engaged suits him."

Emma laughed. "He is rather on top of the moon, I feel envious in a way at least it will be an excellent excuse to do loads of shopping." Her grin widened even further. "We could lash out and go to London, nothing but the best and all that stuff you know."

"I thought that you were meant to be saving, honestly Emma you will never change."

"Money is to spend mother; it's no fun hoarding it away for a rainy day and forgetting about it. Don't be so old-fashioned,

172

you have to live a little and be happy. What shall we do tomorrow?"

I felt my jaw tighten, and felt Emma's questioning eyes upon me. "For a start I am going to be firm with John this evening. I'll tell him that I'm going to have a day with you tomorrow. I'll get his meals done and laid out on the table for him so that he just has to help himself. It will do him no harm to be without anyone for once. He is getting far too spoilt. I deserve a day off, and after all we have only got a couple days left before everyone returns."

Emma smiled. "That's the ticket, mum, you boss John about a bit. It will do him good but make sure you mean it otherwise he will twist you round his finger and make you be with him."

"I'll go and tell him now while I'm on the boil then at least it will be over and done with, then we can plan what to do in the morning. You go on out round the grounds for a bit of fresh air Emma. The lake is nice to walk round at this time of day; if you're quiet you might even catch a glimpse of the otter that John has supposed to have seen, that really would be exciting. In the meantime I will get John sorted out. If when you come back and I'm not about, you can always get on with the vegetables if you're bored." I quickly ducked to miss the book that my daughter had just hurled at me. Laughing, Emma turned on her heel and disappeared.

Briskly I rinsed the odd cup and saucer out, laying them gently on the washboard. One of them was of delicate white china with a beautiful coloured kingfisher on. It looked so real and life-like that for a moment I was spellbound. I felt as though it would fly away at any moment. My gaze turned towards the kitchen window and the garden. I had meant to pick some of the flowers for the vases in the hall, and would have to do those another day. Where on earth had the time gone? As usual it had flown by. I suddenly realised that I was tired. It had not been a rest coming here, as Emma had said everything was taking its toll. I should be with my husband in the West Country saving my marriage if not our cottage. I realised that Broome Cottage would have to be sold. Something inside of me was trying to tell me that if I didn't, I would lose James and that was what I didn't really want.

Dreamily I looked round the old-fashioned kitchen. The floor consisted of old slate tiles with antique pine cupboards on the walls; a tiled table stood near the window looking out onto the vast lawn and grounds beyond. The window was old and the white paint was peeling away in places; a tiny spider was weaving a web in the corner; a dried-out geranium plant stood on the narrow windowsill along with a dish that contained elastic bands, needle and cotton, a lost lonesome button, along with a five and ten pence piece. It was a kitchen that was contented and at peace, no wandering spirit had touched here. It was a room on its own where nothing disturbed it only the wind from the trees and the hooting of owls during the night. Occasionally, the light of a full moon would float serenely through the kitchen windows to rest for a while in its cosiness.

I stood up abruptly, time to get on. It was passing swiftly and I had not even spoken to John yet about the arrangements for the morning.

Hastily I stood up and pushed the kitchen door open, walking briskly through the hall down the little step towards the sitting room and John's study, my mind still on Emma and what we should do tomorrow. Glancing into the sitting room as I passed I saw the evening sun filtering through the windows; the smell of the old worn leather and musty ancient books came to my nostrils. I peeped into the doorway. Rows and rows of books stood upon the shelves stretching right along to the equally old fireplace, a hint of burnt logs filling the room with my favourite scents of logs and books. I tiptoed a little further into the room. This room also looked at peace and very restful. Indeed, the brown leather armchairs looked cosy and inviting. Slowly I picked a book up at random only to hastily put it back onto the shelf; it was not one of my favourite authors. Moving further along the shelf I spied a book with a light green cover with black writing on it, one which looked old and well-worn as though it had been read and enjoyed many times before. My hand eagerly reaching upwards to get it down blowing the dust off, I settled myself down into one of the deep, comfy armchairs and opened it at the first chapter and started to read.

The story made light pleasant reading. After a few pages I started to grow sleepy. The warmth of the sun pleasant on my shoulders, along with the faint sound of birds from the trees and bushes outside, relaxed my mind and body totally. It was what I had needed – a little time to myself – for my mind to wander at its own free will, to capture the sense of freedom, which was at one time mine, would it ever be again?

My mind sleepily turned to James. What was he doing, what was he now thinking, going off to Cornwall without even speaking to me first. I felt deeply hurt and concerned. Had he had enough of everything or had he just had enough and grown tired of me and wanted pastures new in all senses of the word." "Catherine are you there?" John's voice bellowed out from the top of the landing making me jump up in fright, dropping the book with a bang.

As I did so, something fell to the floor. It looked like an old photograph, the print had faintly yellowed with age and the corners were curling slightly as though at one time it had been left in the sun and forgotten.

"Catherine where are you," the voice now sounded cross and tetchy.

I shouted back at the top of my voice, "I'm coming John, just give me a minute and I will be straight up."

Curiously I quickly glanced at the photograph which I still held in her hand. I held it closer; it looked as though it had been taken near the top flight of the steep stairs leading to the rooms and bedrooms above which were the very oldest and creepiest part of the mill. I could just about make out a faint shadow standing outlined near to the top, a figure which I just could not quite make out, as though possibly it was only a shadow. Instantly I froze and immediately knew what it was. This picture which I was holding had been taken in the oldest part of the building which had been originally built in the 12th Century. Looking more closely I could see the faint outline of what looked like a pale long cloak, a figure in a flowing cloak. I could now just about see a pair of eyes in the faint glow of the face. That was it, surely it must be. It could only be the white lady; Watermill Farm did have a ghost after all. Excitedly I looked even more closely at the photograph. Who had taken it and why was it not spoken about? John, I felt sure, knew of its existence. He had muttered her name the night that he had been poorly as though he had seen her that very night; ghosts did indeed exist not only in Broome Cottage but here at the farmhouse as well.

For the third time I looked again at the picture held in my hands. It was definitely at the very top of the stairs. The vague outline of the face staring out at her beyond the photograph looked as though it had been caught unawares; its hands were slightly raised as though in anger at being seen, therefore whoever had taken the picture must have been halfway up. The stairs were extremely steep and wooden ones as well; the ghost must have been coming from the direction of John's bedroom and about to descend the stairs when the picture had been taken, but by whom?

Vaguely I could hear John returning to his room. Feeling a great sense of excitement, I carefully returned the photograph back in the book as I had found it. If I had time I could show it to Emma later on.

I was simply bursting to tell someone what I had just witnessed but commonsense told me to bide my time and wait. John must tell me himself, but how and why would he not speak about it? Was it something to do with his wife? She had been dead a long time, that I did know, but how did she die? The question now seemed important as though there lay an important clue to this ghost, and why did she want to visit the local church? All these questions and no answers were buzzing like bees around my head. John, I must finish John, get his supper, get him to bed so that I can speak to Emma. I must tell someone, all these spirits were getting too much to keep to myself.

I turned and put the book neatly back on the shelf, then slowly my heart still pounding from my exciting find I climbed up the stairs to John.

I flung his bedroom door open wide with a flourish. A chaotic scene met my eyes, trousers, ties, belts were strewn everywhere on the floor and spilling out of his chest of drawers.

"Oh terrific, John," I muttered, this is just what I wanted, "What on earth have you been doing," my voice sounded loud and impatient. It would take ages to put this lot away neatly in their orderly piles where they belonged.

"I am not at all amused John what on earth are you playing at?" He turned round to face me with a bemused expression on his face.

"I have lost my brown tie with the grey spots on, have you seen it anywhere Catherine?" His voice sounded tetchy a bit like mine. "Ahh I can see it," he cried, "it's fallen behind the wardrobe. I can just see the tip of it. I have been searching everywhere for it, be a dear and pull it out for me," poking his stick onto the end of the offending tie just in case it should happen to disappear in front of his eyes. At that very moment the telephone decided to ring. I snatched it up irritably.

"Hello," I shrieked into the phone furiously.

"Oh, um, mum, is that you?" It was Adam, my heart leapt out of my mouth. "Gosh mum it didn't sound like you, are you alright you seem as if you're awfully cross? Have I rung at a bad time?" Silence, tears welled up in my eyes, for a minute I just could not speak.

"No I'm sorry Adam," forcing the tears back quickly I put my hand to my forehead. "No I mean I'm okay, really I am, how are you? This is a surprise I didn't expect to hear from you until the weekend at least."

In one great rush I felt all the pressure and tension of the last few days seep out of me. "I'm fine really fine, but so much better for hearing you. I need to ask you so many questions. Emma has been telling me that your dad is in Cornwall, which I

178

can't really imagine, especially not telling me that he was going. It's not like your father at all to be secretive like that."

I heard in the background John giving a huge sigh and plod off slowly to the bathroom. He had evidently forgotten about his blessed tie.

"It's true mum." Adam spoke quietly. "He just went without any explanation or apology, just plonked the dog down and away he went. He didn't look well at all, just went without even a wave or backward glance. In fact for dad he looked really ill and exhausted."

"Didn't he say anything at all?" I whispered.

"No nothing that made any sense mum, only that he must get away for a while to think. I haven't heard from him since and to tell you the truth I'm a wee bit concerned about him, as you say it is not like him at all."

I chewed my lip apprehensively while I listened. Adam was worried. I was worried, we all were. Thank goodness I only had two more days to look after John. I really could not cope with him anymore.

"If I hear from him I'll let you know immediately Adam, I'll be home in a few days, but I'm sure that he will be back before then." We said our goodbyes. I heard the click of the phone signalling the end of the call. I felt myself still hanging onto the end of the receiver willing Adam to come back, his voice had been such a comfort to me. Unexpected tears once again welled up into my eyes. I heard a voice behind me, a tired voice.

"I still can't reach this wretched tie of mine, Catherine if you have finished on my telephone would you kindly help me get it if you can."

I could hear the slightly sarcastic tone in his voice. Drat the man he was treating me like a servant instead of what I thought I was – a valued friend.

Stooping down I handed him his tie, picking up some trousers as I did so.

"I'll have to clear this lot up in the morning John, it's getting late now and I still have supper to put on. Also whilst I have got your attention, I would like a day with Emma tomorrow, so I'll leave a cold lunch for you so that you can help yourself."

He frowned, but before he could utter a sound I had vanished. Clattering down the stairs, I charged into the kitchen.

Emma glanced up startled. Thankfully I saw that she had prepared the evening meal. "What's up mum you look a bit peeved," her frown deepened as she bit into an apple.

Sliding onto the nearest chair I explained all about the faded photograph that I had found along with Adam's anxious phone call. This was all followed by a pensive silence from both of us, until at last Emma broke into a torrent of words. "Oh Emma please don't quiz me anymore. I know only as much as you do. What we have to try and do this evening is to get John to open up, try and get him to talk about the white lady. I just don't know why he is keeping it all such a big secret."

Emma was staring at me in horror. "It's not true, it can't be true surely there cannot be a live ghost here at Watermill Farm, quick mum where is the photo I must have a look at it now."

"Come with me," I muttered pulling her towards the door. "Five minutes is all I can spare to show you, John will shortly be down for his dinner and it's not even cooking yet."

Dragging the book for the second time from the shelf, I trembled as I opened it up at the first chapter to display the photo and held it out for Emma. I heard her give a gasp as she whipped it from my hand. "Phew mum what a picture," her eyes widening like saucers. "You're so right it is a ghost. I just can't believe it is one. If the newspapers got wind of this all hell would be let loose." The floorboards upstairs started to creak. "That's John, he must be coming down for his supper. Quick put it back before he finds us looking at it."

John is slow, very slow and luckily we were back in the kitchen well before he reached the top of the stairs.

"Come on we must get on with dinner. On second thoughts perhaps we could even show him that photo tonight, just say it fell out of a book."

"That's a good idea mum, if we do that he will have to spill the beans. He must surely know about it."

The following hour dragged by as John took ages eating his supper. "We have got to get together a plan of action," said Emma frantically. "He is so slow tonight, it's unbelievable. How about we cancel our day out in the morning and pretend to him that we are going to spring-clean the sitting room as Maggie never has time to get round to doing it, then we can discover the photo accidentally if you know what I mean." The hesitation must have clearly showed in my face. "Come on mum, we have got to bring this thing to a head and I for one want to know why John will not admit to having a ghost in the house and that we really must find out before we go home."

Excitedly Emma hugged me. "At least something is happening that is different for a change. Life is usually so boring."

We finally managed to get John to bed at long last. We did not waste any more time and hastily climbed the stairs after him to our respective bedrooms.

It had started to rain. I listened to it beating onto the windows. The wind had risen again I could hear the trees and leaves outside whirling about, but tonight I was far too weary to listen to it. I must have fallen into my bed and dropped instantly to a dreamless sleep.

Drowsily I awoke to the pleasant aroma of bacon being fried. Where was I? My mind was blank like a blank page. I struggled hard to remember where I was, who I was. Slowly and dimly it all came back to me.

The bedroom door burst open with a crash. "Come on mother I have done a cooked breakfast especially for you. Do hurry and get up before it spoils." She blew a kiss and was gone.

What on earth had I done to deserve a cooked breakfast? I wondered. It was not at all like my daughter to be cooking for me especially so early in the morning.

Outside the wind and rain had stopped, heralding a fine day to come.

I sprang out of bed, a strange lightness in my heart which I had not had for some time. My early morning feast of bacon and eggs was very enjoyable and I lingered lazily over my freshly made coffee. In fact the whole day turned out to be like a movie picture, everything went just like clockwork.

John was so pleased to discover that he was not going to be left alone in the house. We were to find out later that day and why.

The morning turned out to be manic. Sue Ashcroft, John's wife, rang to say that she would be home the next day, probably early afternoon if she managed to make a good start to the day. I could at last think of going back to my own home, what a pleasant thought that was.

Emma appeared to be in a wicked teasing mood, full of banter and charm coaxing John to eat his breakfast in under an hour instead of the usual three. "You're extremely happy this morning my dear," his eyes took in Emma's bright chirpy voice and twinkling eyes. She had put on bright red lipstick today, with gold loop earrings, a white blouse and a half-length black gypsy skirt.

"Well my dear John," she chirped, "mother and I have decided to clear out your sitting room today. It is simply full of dust. It's untidy and the ornaments need a good wash and the windowsills are full of cobwebs. Maggie just does not have the time, so we thought it would help if we did it, that's okay with you isn't it John, I mean you don't mind if we start on it do you? I'm sure it will keep mother out of mischief if you know what I mean!" giving me an enormous wink out of the corner of her eye, which John could not possibly have seen.

For a moment a look of puzzlement crossed his face. "If that is how you wish to spend your last day here, it's fine by me. Are you alright with that idea Catherine?" I nodded. "It doesn't seem like much fun to me, but there I'm a man," he added looking at us both questionably, as if awaiting a reply.

"It will certainly help Maggie. She has so much to do in this huge farmhouse, and it is in need of a spring-clean. Also I have Emma to help me, though if you could supervise the books John as I don't want to put them in the wrong order."

I felt Emma give me a nudge followed by a giggle. Suppressing a smile, I tried to ignore her and turned to John again.

"I'll just get your herbal tea, while I'm doing that Emma will take you to the sitting room and get you sitting comfortably in your armchair." John shuffled a few steps forward with the aid of his stick, Emma followed him.

I took a while making him his tea. It was pleasant to have time on one's hands if only for a few minutes to dwindle a few seconds away in empty thoughts.

Within a short time I was carrying John's precious mug of tea down the passageway and into the musty room where John was now seated, Emma was near the window. "Just look at these cobwebs on the windowsill. It's really been sadly neglected in this room, don't you think?"

It smelt pleasant enough, but it felt warm and airless. A huge bluebottle buzzed around the lamp which stood on the nearby table and in the far corner of the windowsill an enormous cobweb was studded in dead flies.

"Yuk," said Emma and went to open the window, which seemed to have warped a bit and needed some muscular persuasion from both of us. The bluebottle buzzed away into the open air.

Emma said, "What do we do about the cobweb?"

"Remove it," said John

"What with?" Emma replied.

"I think Maggie keeps the dustpan and brush amongst other cleaning things in the cupboard below the stairs, though it's a long time since I have peeped inside myself. I keep well away from that side of things." John's eyes had lost their shuttered vacant look and had started to twinkle with amusement, then he laughed, "If there is so much as a mouse or a beetle lurking, we will send it on its way that's a promise."

We started with great enthusiasm clearing his large desk, which was full of books and writing material. This was all covered in thick dust, which took us far longer than we had originally thought.

By the time everything had been put back onto the table, John had managed to look through every item before we could throw anything away which was most time consuming, but at long last it was time to take the books down from the shelves. Our time was going to come after all.

"Books so many books, I've always been a collector. Too many books, please, any time, if you want, borrow. Provided of course, you bring it back."

Emma smiled, "I might just do that John, I read far more than mother does and I will bring it back I promise."

"You're clearly an intelligent reader. A girl after my own heart, what else do you like to do besides reading books?"

"Music I simply adore it. You can choose your own mood. My uncle introduced me to music and I have got quite a big collection now."

"Come along daughter," I grumbled, "time to make a start on these shelves. It will be lunch time soon if we are not careful."

The first shelf was easy and not too dirty. The second shelf was packed with books, some leather bound and others with deliciously new shiny jackets, novels and biographies that one longed to read but were not at all easy to get hold of as some were quite large and ancient. This was when John first started to get a little agitated. Emma stood above the fireplace on the stool to reach across to get the books that were in the far corner when suddenly she gave a scream as her foot slipped. She grabbed at the shelf bringing a pile of books down with her as she fell; it looked so convincing that for a moment I really thought that it had been an accident until I saw Emma give me a grin. A pile of books lay in a sad heap on the floor. An ancient photograph had flown through the air from one of them and had landed near to John's foot.

Emma paused seeing the growing horror on John's face.

"I'm so sorry I just somehow missed my footing." Emma's voice sounded full of concern. "I'll pick all the books up, I'm sure that none of them are damaged."

"It does not matter about the books. Are you alright my dear girl, are you hurt at all, would you like a cup of tea?" That was John's answer to everything a cup of tea.

Emma was in the meantime gathering all the books up and laying them in neat piles on the floor. "I'm fine thanks, John, I slipped that's all. I am more concerned about your books that's all as some of them look very expensive ones to me, though I would love a drink in a minute. All of this dust is making me thirsty." Her face suddenly looked curious. "What is that by your foot, John? Here let me pick it up for you." Before he could even turn to look she had swooped down to pick it up, then studied it intently as though seeing it for the very first time.

Emma stuttered, "I really can't see what it is, unless, surely it can't be" she looked at it even more closely "It is, but how, oh goodness, to me it looks like a ghost on the stairs."

At that precise moment John raised his hands in horror then froze. His face had gone deathly white. "Give that to me, it's mine, hand it here to me this instant." His hands were shaking as he reached out to snatch it from her grasp.

Firmly I stepped between them. "Let me have a look first Emma." Quietly and firmly I took it from her grasp, then looking at it as though for the first time I spoke to John. "It is as Emma says it looks like a ghost, John, you must have seen this photograph before. It is after all in one of your best books, you must have seen it before."

He stared long and hard at my face, then he crumbled and started to cry quietly, "What is it John, who is this ghost? Is it who you call the Lady of the Night. If it is, who took the picture, what is the story, why are you so upset by the picture?"

By now John was sobbing and gasping for air, it certainly had been a tremendous shock for him coming out of the blue like this. "Emma go and make him some tea, quickly now he seems to be in shock." She herself took off like a frightened rabbit; I heard her running down the passageway towards the kitchen at top speed.

Gently I took John's hand, I certainly had not meant things to turn out as they had done, certainly not to have got him into this state.

Within a few minutes Emma was back with cup of strong hot tea in her hands. It was several minutes later that John started to recover a little, though still extremely upset, he explained in tiny sentences what had happened so many years ago.

"My first wife Jane, who died ten years ago, believed in the supernatural, ghosts, anything at all in that nature. She had told me so many times that there was a ghost who lived here at Watermill Farm. My wife described her as a tall lady who was always dressed in white." He hesitated and took another sip of tea before going on further. "My wife always used to call her The Lady in White, once my wife died I too had visions of her."

Once again John appeared shaky as though the memories were too much for him. I gently tried to coax him onto going further back in time, while Emma sat on the footstool gazing up at him and doting on every word that he said.

Speaking quietly to him, I asked questionably, "How was the picture taken John who took it?"

"My wife Jane who I loved dearly was a really keen photographer. She always took her camera with her wherever she went. I used to tease her about the white lady saying that the only time that I would believe her would be if she were able to get a photograph of it." His lips trembled at the thought of all this. "It is my fault that she died, all my doing and I loved her so very much."

I could see the perspiration glistening on his face as he spoke. His hands lay trembling in his lap as his vision of things that had happened years ago stirred things up in his mind.

A few more minutes passed while he composed himself then went on.

"The white lady or ghost whatever you like to call it surprised Jane on the top of the stairs. Jane took a picture of it which you have in your hand Catherine. Whilst she was taking it she slipped on the wooden stairs and crashed to the floor below breaking her back in the process. She then died a couple of days later in hospital. Before she died she managed to say that she had taken a picture of the ghost and that it was in her camera. They were the last words that she ever spoke.

I had the film developed but never spoke or showed it to anyone. I believe other people, staff and such like, have perhaps had visions of it. I too have done so on dark stormy nights. It seems to unsettle it for whatever reason that I do not know about, but I will not have ghosts or visions mentioned in this house. My dear wife died through it and through my mockery of it therefore it is not or will not be mentioned in this house again. It is an unhappy ghost, that I know, and it can only be seen by certain people. That is all I know, but the story is forbidden to be spoken about whilst I'm still alive. I was the cause of Jane dying and that is the end to it." He gazed morosely into the fireplace.

He lifted his head up slightly. "There is only one thing that I will add and that is, yes, I am frightened of being left on my own in this house, whether it be day or night. You can tell by the photograph that the ghost did not like having it taken. I am positive that somehow it tripped Jane on the stairs. It did not want to be known and I was the only one that knew about the picture in the camera and sometimes I feel as though the Lady of the Night wishes me to go as I was the only one who knew about her."

John's eyes looked deeply into ours. "No more is to be said of this, do you understand me, do I have both of your promises?"

He sat sleepily in his chair for some time and refused dinner. He was ill and tired. We should not have shown him the photo; he was too old to go back all those years to the pain and sorrow that he had evidently gone through. Best to forget like he said, possibly there were several ghosts here, ones that had latched on to me for whatever reason. All I could do was guess.

We all retired early that night, extremely tired from the day's events. I took John a sweet milky drink up last thing but he had already drifted off to sleep.

Quietly I crept out to my room only to lay awake for hours hoping for the morning to come quickly, as all I now wanted to do was to return home.

I did not have long to wait.

CHAPTER 11

UNSETTLED TIMES

Yesterday had passed so quickly and already felt like a dream. John's wife had so suddenly appeared as if from nowhere without any warning, arriving early to relieve me of my duties.

John that morning had appeared lively and normal as though the events of the day before had already filtered and escaped from his mind.

I had only just finished preparing his breakfast tray, when I heard the back door burst open.

"I'm back I'm home, is anyone about?" I heard Sue shout. Hearing no reply, I could hear her plodding up the staircase towards her husband's bedroom.

Emma burst into the kitchen at the same moment to see what all the noise was about. Within a few minutes Sue was crashing down the stairs to join us, then everyone appeared to be talking at once.

Sue had bought me a huge box of chocolates, along with a lovely scented bunch of flowers and some money tucked inside a pretty card. She appeared so grateful, it somehow made it seem all worth the effort.

We sat round the kitchen table drinking endless cups of coffee. Amongst all the chatter, Maggie the housekeeper rang to say that she would be back the following day. Emma and I exchanged quick glances, which said we might as well go home now while the going was good, which was fine by me. I was aching to get back to my little cottage now. Hopefully when I had a spare minute to gather my thoughts, I would plan a day's outing to London with Emma for a shopping spree – that would be something to look forward to.

We speedily packed our light cases, giving John and Sue a tearful farewell. We would miss John in our own little ways. He was a bit cantankerous but he could be a real dear.

Emma and I had left Watermill Farm at the same time but had planned to meet for lunch in a little restaurant, which was on our way home, just for a little while to make a few plans. It was a pleasant interlude, which went far too quickly. We then said our goodbyes and went on our separate journeys. At last I was home.

I turned the key in the lock; Broome Cottage felt empty and quiet like a shell. I stood deep in thought for a few minutes. I was missing Emma already; her happy laughter and spontaneous chatter were the things I missed most. My brief goodbyes to John were also probably long forgotten. Had all my hard work in helping them out been worth it all? I somehow doubted it very much.

I stepped over a pile of mail. The cottage felt musty and warm. A spider ran across the carpet at top speed used to having its own space this last week.

The light on the answer machine was flashing merrily away, I wondered how many calls I had missed. I twisted my head round to look more closely, six calls it was telling me. I pressed the play button automatically, mainly I suppose, to see if James had left me a message as to why he had gone to Cornwall without telling me.

Adam's was the first message requesting that I ring him upon my return regarding Holly. Of course he would be wanting me to pick her up. It would be good to have her back again, I had missed her.

The second and third message was from my friend wondering when I would be back as she had hoped that I would go to a B.Q. with her at the weekend. Fourth one was a sorry wrong number, five – my panic stricken call which I had left for James, and the last one again for James from his college.

I let out a long sigh, no message from my husband, perhaps he would ring this evening. I hoped so as I wanted to know what was going on. Why had he gone away and more to the point was he going to come back? I just did not know.

I wandered through to the kitchen and opened the back door to let some fresh air in. The light flooded in making things look so much brighter and more cheerful. I could smell the faint scent of roses and honeysuckle drifting in from the garden. A bee buzzed around the outside window and birds chattered away in the bushes. I breathed deeply, that was better. I felt as though things were steadily drifting back to normality.

By the time I had taken my luggage in and unpacked it was late afternoon, time now to go and pick Holly up from my son's. She would be so pleased to see me.

My car started first time as usual, what would I do without it, though it was getting old it never seemed to let me down.

I drove quickly down the road deep in thought and in no time at all I had reached Adam's house. His ancient black car stood in the entrance to his little semi-detached house. I could hear Holly barking noisily from within. Immediately tears of sadness sprang to my eyes, what was happening to my life?

The sound of the front door being wrenched open made me dismiss my sombre thoughts for a while at least.

Holly was already jumping up at me in welcome as though I had been away for months instead of only one week.

Adam stood back surveying the scene with a look of amusement on his face, his lean figure looking the picture of contentment.

"Come on in mother." He smiled warmly then came forward to give me a hug.

Still with Holly leaping with excitement at my heels, we entered my son's modern brightly coloured house, not for him wood burners and sweet smelling oils. It was cold black leather chairs with spotless white rugs on the floor, a few ornaments scattered about here and there, just the basic things which are very typical of a man.

Possibly if he married Carol all of that would change. She like me loved her little bits and pieces around her.

"Come on in mother, have you heard from dad yet? There must be something up for him to go off like that so suddenly." He looked at me in a quizzical fashion. "You're not splitting up, are you?"

I hurriedly went through to his kitchen. "I really don't know Adam, I wish that I did. Are you making coffee as I don't think my brain will work unless I have one?"

Gratefully I sank into his one and only really comfortable chair. His other ones were so hard, or was it a sign that I was feeling my age?

Adam spoke in hushed tones.

"Mother you just can't go back and sleep in that cottage on your own especially as dad is not there at the moment," I heard his voice grow louder, "where the devil is he, mum? Why hasn't he made a telephone call or made contact somehow? Whatever has made him go off like this and how come it's all gone so far without either of you telling us anything?"

Adam was quiet while he filled the kettle and sorted the cups out. He knew how fussy I was. I liked the bone china ones with thin edges, not the horrible thick ones that clung to your lips like rubber.

It wasn't until I had my hot cup of coffee in my hand and Holly lying contentedly by my side that he spoke.

His eyes making contact with mine, "I know something is going on mother and I don't yet know what it's all about but my hunch is that it is serious and it's about time that you spilled the beans. Emma says that ghostly things have been happening at Broome Cottage but that you won't go into it with her, and you must know why dad has gone away without a word to any of us."

I felt his hand hold mine tightly; then again he whispered, "You must tell me mum and now, come on." This time he spoke more urgently his eyes full of concern and so anxious to help. The shutters that I had held fast for so long suddenly crumbled along with all my composure. My face dropped its mask and I cried, letting release some of the tension and sadness that was within me.

Once my sobbing had ceased, I felt able to go on. I told my son simply and clearly what had been happening, straining far into the depths of my mind as to when the spirit had first visited me. How it would not appear at first when James was about, then eventually to how the spirit had turned and made itself aggressively known to James. The turning point, for the worst, was when the presence had wanted me to itself – that was when the real problem had started. James was scared really scared. Adam listened intently, not interrupting at any time, only the tightening of his hands on mine and the occasional intake of breath told me that he couldn't quite take all of this story in. It took a long while to tell my son everything in detail as it had happened. Once I had finished we both sat in exhausted silence for a few minutes. I glanced through the kitchen window, seeing the advancing twilight creeping swiftly through the windowpanes. The few odd rays of sun that were left seemed to swiftly fade into the shadows beyond.

Adam dropped his head into his hands then raised it slowly. "I really don't understand. Did you think we would not believe you? These things go on all the time. You read it in the newspapers; magazines are full of it. Things of the supernatural are happening and being televised all the time, so we simply have to find an answer, mum, and soon."

He broke off looking and feeling as shattered as I felt.

I didn't know what to say. He was right of course. Why we had not told him or Emma seemed now a mystery to me. It would have been so much simpler, instead of it all ending like this, possibly even they would have helped us find an answer before now. I felt I must say something to ease this awful tension that was now sitting between us.

"I need to go back home tonight Adam. I only have tomorrow off, then I'll be back to work. I'm sure the spirit won't hurt me Adam I just know it. I won't come to any harm on my own."

Even as I said those words I felt deeply frightened, as one moment everything is peaceful, then as if by magic the spirit reappears from nowhere. I say that I am safe there on my own but can I be sure. I feel my lips tremble slightly at the thought of it. Again Adam broke into my line of thoughts.

"I repeat again," his voice was even louder this time. "You are not going home alone is that perfectly clear?"

Silence invaded the kitchen for a few seconds. He then swiftly knelt down on the floor beside Holly and gently stroked her head then buried his face into hers, a sure sign that he was most upset.

My whole body ached with tension. I reached for the dirty cups and made my way to the sink reaching automatically for the washing up liquid.

I heard Adam stir. "I'll pack a quick overnight bag and come back home with you and stay the night until dad returns."

An overwhelming feeling of relief surged through my veins; perhaps at long last whichever path things took the saga would at last come to a final end once and for all. It could not be too soon to my way of thinking. I felt better already.

It did not take long for Adam to pack a few bits and pieces.

"It will be better if we take our own vehicles mum, then tomorrow I can come back when I'm ready. Is that okay?" he questioned.

"That's okay by me," I replied lightly, "see you back at the cottage."

He kept within easy distance of me as though he did not want to lose sight of me. By the time we got back to the cottage it was more or less dark. The outline of the woods beyond looked and felt welcoming. There was no presence here tonight, that I felt sure of, even though the cottage now was in complete darkness. No lights anywhere to be seen which meant still no James. My heart sank, was this to herald a new life on my own?

"Come on, mother, there's no time to stand and dream." There was a slight edge of impatience to his tone. Guiltily I spun round I was spoiling his weekend, perhaps he would have been meeting Carol but for me.

I hurriedly groped around for the keys in my bag, in the bottom as usual. Holly was already happily chasing ahead to the front door pleased to be home at last.

The key turned swiftly and silently into the lock. My hand fumbled for the light switch in the hall, my eyes glancing towards the answering machine. It was flashing two calls. My heart leapt. Would one of them be from my husband?

"Go straight through make yourself at home," I called. "The spare bedroom has got clean sheets on the bed. Have you had any supper yet?" my eyes darting round as I spoke, looking for shadows in the corner, reaching out all my vibes and feelings for anything strange.

It felt empty I breathed a sigh of relief. Everything was as it should be but would it have been if Adam had decided to stay in his own home tonight – that I would never know.

I heard movements in the kitchen, plates being put out, drawers being opened and shut again quickly.

"I'm just getting a few things ready for supper, mum, then I'll just check the rooms first just to make sure that everything is in order. Then I will do us an omelette, if you like, as I'm feeling quite hungry. You must be too."

I was already turning to the answering machine as he was still speaking. I pushed the knob down for the first fresh message.

"Hi, it's James here."

I stopped dead in my tracks to listen more carefully.

"Just a word to see if you are back home yet," a pause while he waited for a reply.

"Evidently not, I'll be home on Sunday, Catherine. Don't know a specific time yet. See you when I arrive whatever time that is, speak to you later."

Emma's was the second message.

"Hello Mother just rang to see how you are. I bet that you're round that brother of mine picking up doggie. Give us a ring when you can, love you lots bye."

I stood and replayed the messages once again. No I hadn't missed any, it was now Saturday evening, tomorrow would be Sunday.

I saw Adam standing at the top of the staircase looking down on me.

"Did you hear those messages?" I questioned.

"Yes I did. Perhaps we can now get his all sorted out when he arrives back home. You might possibly have to sell up that would probably be the best answer, but then did you not say that the presence followed you to Cornwall that time when you went on holiday?"

Tight-lipped I nodded.

"I have had enough for tonight Adam. I feel utterly drained, let's have our meal, get cleared up and forget all about this wretched business for a little while at least."

It was hard to sleep that night. I tossed and turned, fetched a glass of water, looked out of the window, then climbed back into bed and tried once more to get to sleep.

When I closed my eyes, the evening, which I had spent with Adam, came flying back to me like a film playing over and over in my head. My mind would not be stilled.

When at last morning came, I felt tired and depressed. My son too looked strained and weary, though he insisted that he had slept well that night, but he always took the ace card at convincing people.

At least the morning heralded a good sunny bright day ahead. Straight after breakfast Adam had gone into the garden to dig some vegetables up. Ever since our Essex days no matter how busy our days were, we had always tried to keep a small crop of seasonal things growing. We felt it was lovely at the weekends to fetch your own produce from the garden.

It was good to have my son around for a while. We had already decided yesterday to ask Emma over as well. It was now a family matter. My daughter would have to be told as soon as possible even before her father arrived on the scene.

A bunch of dirty fresh carrots suddenly landed on the kitchen table scattering dirt and earth everywhere all over the clean table. I felt a twinge of annoyance. "I'll see if there is anything else to be picked," he shouted then disappeared in search of other things for the feast.

My train of thoughts broken, I irritably grabbed a small knife from the kitchen drawer and started absentmindedly to scrape, my mind still elsewhere. The knife was sharp. I felt the painful stab immediately, blood rapidly seeping out along the edge of my hand dripping into the sink below.

"Blast," and "Blast," again I cursed. "Adam quickly!" I shouted. "Can you help me with these plasters?"

Silence, I shouted again more loudly this time.

"Adam can you hear me?" Still no response, snatching at the tea towel to stem the flow, I stepped out into the garden beyond.

My son had his back to me, his head studying intently the bedroom window, which was immediately above the cellar.

He stood as though rooted to the spot. As I approached nearer to him his head still did not turn to look round. He didn't even seem to hear me though he turned at the sound of my voice again. He looked at me strangely. I wished that he would say something but he simply looked dazed for a minute, then suddenly he seemed to shake himself.

"There is something up there mother, in that bedroom. I saw it move by the window. I saw it watching me. I'm going up there right now, wait here until I return."

That wasn't a sentence it was an order.

Adam ran back into the kitchen. I could faintly hear his feet running up the stairs

Then silence. Exasperated I stood there awaiting his return, looking down at the red stained tea towel in my hand, my finger throbbing. All at once the wind turned unexpectedly and it felt cold. I could hear the laboured thumping of my own heart and I started violently to shiver. Within a few minutes I heard my son enter the kitchen and come back out into the garden. His face looked puzzled.

"There is nothing there, the room is completely empty." His eyes darted above to the bedroom again.

"I know something was up there, it was there at the window and I'm sure that it was looking at me. There is a presence in the house I could feel it as I went up the stairs or what is the other word they call it – an entity?"

He briefly glanced at me. "You have to move from here. Things are not normal at all. It could even be dangerous to keep living here. What did you come out for anyway?"

I waved my hand in front of him.

"A plaster is all I wanted," trying hard to ease the tension as I said it.

"At this rate there will be no dinner ready for anybody."

Nothing more was said. Dinner was eventually bubbling merrily away on the stove and hunger pains were already attacking my stomach or were they purely caused by nerves.

The sound of footsteps and laughter broke into my train of thoughts. Emma burst in through the door. At least one of the family had arrived, but what of her father? Where was he? Would he appear or not? Worriedly I pushed that thought to the back of my head.

"Hi mum, how are you and where has that no good brother of mine disappeared to?"

Hands on hips her eyes darted round.

"I'm here, sister darling." Adam had stepped quietly in. "Come on give us a big hug, there's a good girl." He held out his arms and gave her a vice-like hug. They always had been close even as young children.

"What's for dinner, mother?" My daughter pouted. "I'm starving as usual."

We ate our meal amidst much chatter and laughter, but still no James.

Emma suddenly became subdued, "Where is father, I thought he was supposed to be home by now?"

She gazed at both of us. "Is there anything wrong? You both look as though you are hiding something."

I caught Adam's glance, now must be the time to say our piece. Quietly Adam spoke.

"Shall I tell her, mum? She has got to know. It's no use waiting for dad to turn up. He might not arrive for ages yet."

Hesitantly I nodded, my stomach instantly contracting with nerves. I heard the clock in the hall chime the hour – precisely three in the afternoon – that was the exact time that we had moved into Broome Cottage, so many years ago from Essex.

We had arrived here with our two young children, three dogs, and one cat, all of us tired, hungry and excited.

I remember we had sat in the afternoon sunshine calling loudly to the children not to get lost and them singing all sorts of silly nonsense, our voices echoing throughout the empty house, stumbling upon new finds in the house and garden.

We had run round until we were all out of breath. The first tangs of autumn in the air, swallows had wheeled and swooped high in the sky above us. We then closed our eyes and told our two young children to sit still and listen to the silence of the countryside. They sat down beside us and listened.

I had loved this place from the start. So had my husband but never so much as me.

I remembered Adam finding some black insects among the ivy leaves growing on the garden wall. He had been so excited and had pulled out a handful of the leaves to show us. Possibly he had only been about seven years of age. Where had all the years gone?

I remembered stripping the wallpaper off in the lounge and the slight rustling noise that I had heard and thinking possibly that it was a mouse. Had it then been followed by a squeak. It had all happened such a long time ago that the memory of it all is fading. Perhaps it had been the first movement of the spirit stirring who knows all that time ago.

What had I got left after all those years? – two very capable children, a grown-up young lady and gentleman, one dog and one cat, possibly no husband, my thoughts now returning to the present moment. I could vaguely hear Adam still explaining about the sinister happenings to Emma, her face already looking pensive at the thought of what had been happening in this cottage that she too loved so dearly.

I felt again an intense feeling of overwhelming tiredness in my whole being. My eyes started to close, my body wanted to drift off into a heavenly sleep where no thoughts or memories would trouble me.

A voice that sounded angry broke into my slumbers, which stirred the embers of my heart.

CHAPTER 12

THE MOVE

"It's about time all of this was out in the open!"

James's tall frame stood standing in the hallway. How long he had stood watching I could not imagine. He had entered quietly and stealthily as though his conscience was guilty of some deed or thought that he still had to do.

Typically it was my daughter who spoke first, her voice cold and slightly raised.

"How on earth could you go and leave poor mother to come back home here to this haunted place entirely on her own?"

"Believe me Emma I didn't even want to come back here. In fact I very nearly didn't. It was only the thought of your mother that forced me to return. I hate it here it's evil, and if you knew all what has been going on here you would feel the same."

It was Adam's turn now.

"We have been told everything that has happened right from start to finish, nothing has been left out. I am just so appalled that this has been going on for so long and neither of you have told us. Why the big secret? It's nothing to be ashamed of. It just happens. It's through no fault of yours, and why disappear down to Cornwall at the last minute and being so secretive about it? Mother has been sick with worry, it's just not like you dad not like you at all."

Wearily as though he was thoroughly exhausted, James sank into the nearest chair.

"Is there some coffee going or some water, it has been a long journey?" All was silent until a cup was put in his hand. He then hesitantly carried on.

"When your mother decided to stay at Watermill Farm for a few days I had fully reconciled myself to that fact. However what I had not bargained on was being forced out of my own home by a force that I just could not cope with." His hand went shakily to his lips while he had a few more sips of coffee. This action seemed to give him the strength to continue.

"I have felt utterly terrified many times here in this cottage." His eyes turned to each one of us in turn.

"In fact I can truthfully say that I am lucky to still be alive. The spirit or ghost form that lives now in this cottage to my way of thinking for whatever reason worships your mother and seems to be getting more and more possessive of her with every day and week that passes. I am positive that she is not in danger from it, but I definitely am, it pursues me whenever I'm alone here and it purely and simply wants me out of this cottage and far away. You have been listening to your mother's side of the story, now it's your turn to listen very carefully to mine."

My husband's face looked as though it had been carved from a piece of granite. He looked so solemn and grim that again my stomach knotted up for the bad news which I felt sure was going to come.

His story was so much more convincing than mine. He told it with honesty, clarity and truthfulness and with amazing accuracy in detail, timing and dates, the movements, the shadows on the stairs, the obnoxious smell animating from the source itself, and so he went on going through the things, that I had even forgotten. There was just so much to tell, the time ticked relentlessly away, well past tea-time and James was still remembering things: the tearing up of the floorboards, the sound of a man's boots walking steadily across the room until they came to rest beside my bed and the tapping on the windowpane outside. The story went on and on until eventually there was nothing more left to tell.

I have never ever before sat in such stony silence. We were all speechless with emotion and shock.

We heard James's voice speak again, even his lips did not appear to be moving. His voice though was soft and cold as though every inch of feeling had been whipped from his entire body.

"I went down to the West Country solely to get away from this cottage and to think as to what I should do and do you know why I did that?"

He hesitated for a few brief moments as if struggling deeply with his inner emotions.

"I have now made my decision and that decision though I wish with all my heart that it could be otherwise is that I am going to leave the cottage and sadly your mother. It isn't that I have stopped loving her because I still do. It is because I love her that I have to leave. Whilst I'm with her the presence will keep with us forever and that will eventually destroy both of us."

We all heard a sob pass his lips, then resolutely he carried on.

"Since I have made this decision to go, the presence has gone entirely from my life. It just is not there, gone completely. I feel no shadow by my side, no presence nothing at all. Somehow it knows that I am leaving Broome Cottage and your mother. It now has no reason to persecute me and it does not have to contend with me anymore as my decision is final and nothing will ever make me change it."

The silence that followed grew longer and longer. No one knew what to say or do. Everyone simply knew that I was the only one that could sort this problem out and that no amount of comfort would help. I felt so gutted and heartbroken to even cry. My body was shaking in total disbelief.

This was the news that I had been dreading. I had felt it gently simmering for months until the pot had eventually reached boiling point and exploded.

I felt like screaming, kicking, shouting, 'don't leave me. How can I cope without you?' But no sounds passed from within my lips. I tried to but my lips seemed frozen with this most recent blow that had been dealt.

My time would come later on to lash out at James. I knew that, I needed time to recoup a little of my strength for the blow that my husband had cast, it was indeed a bitter one.

Adam and Emma sat as though deaf and dumb, too scared to be shocked even to utter one syllable. How would I cope in this cottage on my own? How would I feel at night? Would the spirit come and sleep in my bed in place of James without my even knowing it? The thought was repugnant. It did not contemplate thinking of and what was I doing to let my husband go like this?

Numbly my tearful voice broke the silence.

"What if I call the clairvoyant to visit again? She was able to get rid of it before for a while perhaps she can do it again, possibly even to make it go forever?"

My wretchedness hung like a damp towel on a washing line. The devastation that I was feeling at that moment was unbelievable. Nobody could possibly know fully what my feelings were, it was a nightmare that was never ending and should never have begun.

I heard James speaking, he sounded normal again.

"That would be an excellent idea, Catherine, to call out the clairvoyant. What was she called? Oh yes! Amidyne, that was it. I remember now, it sounded such a pretty name. Yes definitely that's a good idea as you will need to have control of the spirit if you stay here in this cottage."

Thoughtfully he looked at the wall opposite as though miles away and into another world.

"I will keep here for a further month. Then I'll go. I am starting a completely new life in the north of Cornwall, though needless to say I will keep in close contact with all of you. You're still my family and my life and nothing ever will alter that fact."

The telephone in the hall started to ring. It kept on ringing but nobody had the inclination to answer it.

"Get the clairvoyant to visit again by all means but my thoughts will not change. You have the option Catherine of selling up this cottage and going your own way or simply to keep this as your home. If you sell up I think in some way this presence will follow you. Not in such a destructive and frightening way as it has done but in a strange way it will be there – a presence or figure perhaps in the faintest of shadows to watch over you. It loves you Catherine and I feel deep down in my bones that it will keep with you always. There explains the reasons why I must sadly break up our marriage."

His voice faltered and tears welled up into his eyes.

"I am so very sorry."

With that he stumbled out into the garden.

I glanced at Adam and Emma. Their eyes too were brimming full of tears along with mine. Our lives would never be the same again.

We hugged each other tightly and firmly so close that we could hear our hearts beating. Suddenly, through our emotion we heard a sound like the cellar door shutting firmly but quietly, as though someone contented with what he had done had closed the door on us all knowing that he was safe to rule the cottage as his. Who of course but the spirit of Broome Cottage?

There was nothing more to be said.

My son and daughter left slowly and sadly. Neither one of us could really believe that our marriage of so many years had come to an end, all because of a force, a spirit, a ghost, whatever one liked to call it, had entered the cottage.

I answered Emma vaguely as though in a trance.

"Yes Emma I will ring up the clairvoyant first thing in the morning. I'll ring work and say that I am unwell, but I will say this – there is no way that I will be able to live here on my own. I would be scared witless, and your father will need part of the money to set himself up somewhere again."

My voice was already shaking with emotion. Was this really happening to me? Please let it be an awful nightmare, where one would wake up in one's own bed warmly and snugly to find that it had all been a bad dream.

My son and daughter both left without even saying goodbye to their father. It was by now getting dark and James was still in the garden somewhere.

Holly wanted a run and my mind was in a complete turmoil. How was I to survive on my own? Where could I go or move to? If I went back to my old home town of Essex it would mean leaving my family and friends and that I could not do. They were all that I had left.

Without hearing a sound, I felt an arm being put around my shoulders; silently James had left the garden and entered the kitchen. I felt the pressure of his body onto mine, and for one fleeting brief silly moment I thought that all was well again with us, but like a piece of broken glass it shattered into a hundred tiny pieces.

"I'm so very sorry, Catherine, with all my heart I didn't want this to happen. I too will have to find a new life and hopefully happiness again. It will be new routes for both of us, but it is entirely up to you whether you stay here on your own or sell up. It will be your decision only. It can only be made by you."

I felt him stroking my hair trying in his way to gently calm me. My sobs started to flow, quietly at first then in gasping torrents, until at last they gradually started to subside.

"It's getting late now, my suggestion is let's both get ready for bed. We are both extremely tired and exhausted; once the morning comes we hopefully will see our position in a more clearer light. Things won't change we both know that, but I have to go you do realise that don't you, Catherine, as I said earlier I will help and protect you as much as I am able to until you yourself know what the future holds."

He kissed me lightly on the cheek and turned towards the stairs.

That night was the longest one of my entire life. James slept with me but there was no warmth and no contact. I felt his body beside mine. We both knew already we were miles apart from each other. He would help me, yes, help steer me through these bad times until a solution had been found, both of us knowing we had lost each other forever.

It was a full moon that night. Its beam shone through the chink in the curtains as though it was daylight outside. Restless I carefully eased myself out of bed and padded to the window.

Everywhere was still; the night sky was alight with stars. No wind stirred among the trees and all of the forest life stood silent as a tomb.

Finally in the early hours of the morning I must have fallen into a deep exhausted sleep, and awoke to the sounds of Holly whining in the kitchen below.

Sleepily I glance at my watch. It was already ten in the morning, my mind instantly flashing back to yesterday, my heart sinking at the thought of the day and weeks ahead.

There was a note that had been placed on my dressing table, as I opened it I knew that it would be from James. It read as follows:

Dear Catherine, I will ring your work this morning to say that you're not well and won't be in for the next couple of days. Remember to get in touch with Amidyne, speak to you tonight. All my love James.

Tears threatened to storm their way through again. I heard Holly whine again. Hurriedly I found my dressing gown and went down the stairs to let her out into the garden. That task completed I poured myself a glass of homemade slow gin. It slid down my chest like fire straight onto an empty stomach. I burped several times and tried hard to think rationally and sensibly. It was indeed a difficult task to accomplish that morning.

Breakfast, bath, then ring Amidyne, the clairvoyant, all in that order if possible. Feeling that my mind was a little more organised I started to feel slightly more optimistic.

James rang, Emma rang, Adam rang – they each had the same question. Was I alright, had I rung you know who yet? I answered all their questions as though in a stupor. I say stupor as I was already on my third glass of gin. It helped to deaden the pain that I was feeling deep inside of me, but would it ever ease I doubted it very much?

As though on autopilot I made dinner for James and myself – Shepherd's Pie that was my husband's favourite. How long would I call him that I wondered, as I boiled the potatoes for the topping?

He arrived home late that evening. His meal was burnt and crusty. He appeared not to mind as he eagerly ate it all up, or possibly he dare not do otherwise.

I told him that Amidyne would be coming on Thursday of this week, but that I had arranged not to be there with her. I had not the strength to go through all of it again. She would have the cottage to herself for a while. Let her discover any hidden forces that lay deep within the cottage wall in my absence.

I did not care anymore it was as simple as that. She would undoubtedly let me know of anything that she discovered.

The following day I did not even attempt to go in to work, my head ached. I felt numb to the bone, exhausted and sad.

James had left early that morning; his face had looked strained and pale. His used coffee cup lay on the draining board. Apart from that it looked as though he had given breakfast a miss completely that day.

The cottage felt empty except for Holly following me about. It felt like an empty shell – nothing left except thoughts and memories.

The day went slowly. Emma rang at lunch time, but the conversation I felt was stilted. She was uneasy, in fact lost for words is the correct phase. She knew that I was unhappy therefore in turn it made her equally so.

James arrived home on time that evening. I had been down to the shops that afternoon and had been tempted to buy a cheese and onion quiche from the local bakery. James took a bite and praised it, then said it was not nearly as light as when I made my own. I was severely tempted to throw it at him.

"Well we are a fine pair," I said lightly. "We need some friends round to cheer us up."

He hung his head and spoke so sorrowfully that he seemed ashamed.

"It's a sad time for both of us. We seem to be in another world to what we were." He shivered. "I really don't know if we will ever be truly happy again. I hope so for both our sakes. We won't know of any outcome until the clairvoyant gives us her opinion which fortunately will not be long now."

A few minutes of deep silence fell between us both.

"Do you think that you will you be returning to work in the morning?"

My husband spoke without interest or feeling. Rapidly blinking back the tears I nodded.

"I had better return and show willing. I suppose they will be wondering what on earth is the matter." I pondered for a few moments.

"I am just getting more and more depressed by the day staying here at home on my own. I'm tired. In fact tired is not the right word I'm utterly exhausted, worn out ready for the rubbish heap. My dread is having to leave this cottage or even to stay in it without you. Either way it fills me with dread. My only real wish is to have my life back to how it was before all of these awful things happened and most of all how will I manage without you?"

Noisily I fled from the room to the bedroom where my whole body shook with heart-rending sobs; the only difference was that James did not come in to comfort me.

I was alone, utterly and completely alone, even the spirit had disappeared and left me. In a way it was laughable that I should be so terribly alone.

Being back at work the next day helped me a little. It was frantically busy and I did not have a chance to brood, be sad or to even think of home. There was another form of life which was called work. It had always helped in the past and it would now do so again along with my prayers for strength and guidance in paths not as yet decided upon.

My lunch break consisted of frantically trying to catch up with some of my work, invoices and statements that should have been sent out over a week ago, time now to speedily try and catch up.

Adam had invited us all round to his house that evening for a Chinese meal. He knew how I loved them, so a sense of normality would prevail for a while if only for one evening for which I was grateful.

We were both glad to get out of the house that evening. Amidyne would be visiting the next morning. A lot would be depending upon what she told us.

The Chinese meal was excellent and everyone made light conversation ignoring the topic of Broome Cottage altogether, so it all went off quite pleasantly. We finished it off by having several games of cards which eased the strain of any awkward silences.

Neither of us spoke on the way back home that evening. It was a blustery night and we were both deep in our own thoughts. James had now gone to sleeping in the spare bedroom. The decision had been his not mine, and I felt lonelier than ever before in my life.

At last Thursday morning had arrived. I felt a feeling of nervousness, eagerness, expectancy of something which could be of major importance to happen, a case of going forward and not back, simply a case of no return. What would be would be, as the saying goes. There was now no turning back.

Surprisingly I now wanted to stay at home to see Amidyne in and to hear what her visions and sightings were, but instinct told me to head for work for I would soon know the outcome of her visit. She would be here again very soon on Saturday morning, Adam and Emma would be with me, but not James he had told me he had affairs to attend to that day that could not be possibly postponed. I thought what a load of old bull he was telling me.

Upon my return late in the afternoon after my day at work, I turned into our little cottage and wondered what awaited me.

Alone I entered the warm kitchen. There on the table was a small printed blue and white card with the clairvoyant's name printed clearly on it and in spidery tiny cobweb handwriting she said that she had called at such and such a time and that she would come to see us on Saturday at ten in the morning to discuss her findings. I turned the card over. There was not even a clue or a hint to whether she had been in touch with the spirit or even seen it. The card felt cold and ominous.

Shakily my hands turned to put the card up on the mantelshelf for my husband to read. It slipped from my hands like a speck of dust. Was that an omen for me to move, or was that a figment of my now vivid imagination? No doubt I would soon know.

The headlights of James's car flashed past the kitchen window. I heard his door slam. I would miss him when he eventually left for good. I pretended to be busy when he opened the back door. I would act as coldly as he was doing, for tonight anyway.

Saturday I rose early. James had risen even sooner as though intending to completely miss me. He had left a note in the bathroom which had simply said good luck with one solitary kiss at the end of it. Tears threatened to engulf me once more; bravely I tried to push them back.

As I slipped down stairs I found that Holly was still sound asleep in her basket. I reached up to the shelf for the coffee jar.

My dog and drinking endless cups of coffee appeared to be the only stability that I had in my life at the moment. I looked out of the window to a bleak morning. For a brief moment I felt a hand touch my shoulder and hair. I spun instantly round to find that there was no one there. Shakily I turned the other way. Holly had awoken and was whining at the door. Her hackles were rising on her back, and her whole appearance was extremely agitated. The air had turned chilly with a hint of mustiness in the air. Suddenly I felt faint and sick; I heard once again the door of the cellar closing quietly.

Who had touched my body? Was it a form of comfort made by George or was it another spirit that had entered this cottage; I felt rooted to the spot.

Automatically my hand reached for the radio, my scalp tingled some form of force was still about. My mind was suddenly made up. There was no way that I could stay on my own in this cottage. I would have to sell up no matter what the clairvoyant advised me to do. It would be the house that stood alone until a new owner had been found.

Trembling I glanced at my wristwatch, only just two hours before Adam and Emma arrived and three before the clairvoyant. I had more than enough time to take the dog for a long energetic walk, and to get away from this eerie haunted cottage for a while.

Exhausted after my walk with the dog, the doorbell finally rang at the front door. Two rings that would be Adam, he usually was the first one to arrive. Emma arrived late as always, somewhat like her mother in that respect.

After a brief discussion we decided to sit and gather round the old and ancient pine table in the dining room. The atmosphere was good in there and it was warm. The early morning sun filtered gently through the windows. We then gathered the brown and white spotted mugs from the kitchen to make the table look homely. A false air of cheerfulness hung about us as though getting ready for the storm to break.

I had made a batch of fruit scones the evening before, so I quickly warmed them in the oven to give the house a lovely aroma of fresh baking.

At last Amidyne arrived. I was nervous. What had she found out? Had she managed to contact the spirit? I steeled myself and hesitantly got up from my chair to let her in.

She was friendly as before, though to my mind faintly reserved, filling in with small talk as she drank her coffee. Adam and Emma instantly liked her. I could tell by their faces and body language.

As if by an invisible being all was unexpectedly quiet, we sat patiently and waited.

I watched Emma nervously biting her lip. I sniffed and wished Amidyne would hurry up and tell us what was happening.

The clairvoyant's deep dark penetrating eyes stared straight past the dining room doors and into the hallway and stairs beyond.

"You do have a presence in this cottage. It was here when I visited on Thursday and it is here with us again now."

The air prickled with anticipation. I then heard faint footsteps up in the room above. My daughter looked at me as though she had heard it too. No one else seemed aware of it.

Emma's hand pressed tightly into mine, and Adam cleared his throat as though wishing he were somewhere else.

The clairvoyant then spoke as though speaking through someone else.

"The spirit or force, whatever you like to call it, usually waits and listens on the top landing as it is now. This force is a strangely obstinate one who believes that this cottage is still his home as, once many moons ago, it was."

"The spirit keeps insisting that you, Catherine, are his wife and that he died in this cottage when his wife was still alive. His death happened in the cellar underneath the stairs and as you know, his name is George.

221

"There is also another force that has just recently departed from this earth plane and now visits this cottage frequently. She says that her name is Alice."

Amidyne looked at us in silence for a few seconds as though the name should mean something to us all.

I shuddered. Was that whom I had felt earlier in the kitchen, but who was Alice? It somehow rang a bell as though I had heard the name before somewhere.

Nobody could answer her question, puzzled I shook my head.

"The second presence, which you have visiting here." She paused, the clairvoyant's eyes were now looking directly into mine, "belongs to George's real wife, Alice.

"Now that she has passed from this earth world, she wishes him to be on the second galaxy with her where he should rightly be. Even though George had entered this same galaxy for a while several years earlier, for some reason he had not been able to settle like the other spirits. This can happen occasionally when we exit the earth hurriedly like he did. He missed his wife so much at that time, or so the heavenly forces have told me."

Amidyne paused to sip her coffee slowly, then gently continued.

"According to the spirit world something extraordinary happened at the time when George could not settle on the second galaxy. Sometimes if there is a lot of spiritual activity in a certain area this can cause an ancestral happening which is a brightly coloured beam like a brilliant shining rainbow in the sky. This can appear with white glassy mountains in the distance. The forces say that this is a true apparition of life on the other planes and galaxies."

Amidyne sat motionless for a few minutes dreamily looking into space as though she were seeing many visions and faces. Her lips were making movements as though she were talking to the spirits.

Glancing at her anxiously I ventured to ask whether she would like another drink. She chose to ignore this question or else she was so far into her other world that she did not hear me.

"This apparition is haunted by spirits of the second galaxy. These spirits of the second galaxy have the option to keep on the plane where they are to live in peace or they may follow this ancestral light in spirit form back to the earth. This brilliant beam fell over part of Shropshire including this cottage where George had lived for many years in his lifetime and where you are now living.

"I have made contact with George again for him to return to the inner galaxies as his wife has been waiting for him. She has now left this earth plane and has entered the spirit world and beyond. She wishes him to join her but George is reluctant to go, as in his spirit world he has grown to love you Catherine as you are so much like his wife. He thinks that you are his wife. He has always loved living here in this cottage. He had evidently lived here many years before his death and even though he has gone to the land of spirit he is content here with you, so that he does not wish to leave and will possibly stay in this cottage forever.

"I have told him that he must go back to the galaxy that he was on, then that would make Alice contented as she has been waiting for him to join her and she is getting angry because he prefers you now. Therefore this spirit of Alice is showing her presence in this cottage too."

Amidyne face looked restless again as though she were talking to someone beside her.

"I realise that this is an awful lot for you and your family to take in. I have spoken to many spirits and know this to be true. George may leave next month, next year, perhaps never. My views are that we will never know for sure, but it could happen that one day he will wish you to join him in the spirit world, and in that case he might even try to arrange your death making it of course look accidental, so that you can both enter the second galaxy together.

CHAPTER 13

SELLING UP

We all drank coffee in silence, the scones untouched on the table. I stiffly got to my feet and went to open the kitchen door breathing the deep clean air into my nostrils, the sharp early twinges of autumn making me shiver.

I heard Emma say shakily:

"What do you advise my mother to do? Dad is leaving her but you probably know that already. What I'm trying to say is it safe for her to stay here alone or should she move away and will it then follow her?"

The silence before she answered was long, far too long. I came back and sat down at the table. My nerves were taut and raw. I did not really know where I wanted to move to, I just knew that I would now have to definitely sell up. I could not risk having to live with this spirit, George, for the rest of my entire life. I could not stand it and would not.

The cottage somehow now felt completely desolate; it contained happy memories which were now past and gone.

I felt Amidyne watching me closely. She then gently took hold of my hand and whispered:

"Think very carefully, Catherine, you will not be on your own if you stay here. This force is not like the usual ones that I have come across. It is strong, fierce and possessive. I cannot deal with it like I should. This one it is far different from the rest and has a sense of evil about its form. It has lived here with you too long now. It really believes that you are his wife."

Adam let out a low whistle and spoke crossly.

"There surely must be some way of getting rid of the wretched thing. What about a priest blessing the house or getting rid of it like you did before. Surely anything is worth a try."

Amidyne spoke so quietly that we all had to strain our ears to hear what she said.

"I have just told you that this is no usual force. If I persevere with trying to remove it, then we are all at risk of it entering our bodies and doing further damage. It is not of the usual form. You Catherine should decide to move away from this cottage. You must go right away and live in a completely different part of England. You must remember as the ancestral beam shone over this side, it means that this particular area is one of the most haunted parts of Britain, haunted by spirits of the second galaxy.

"The decision must be made by you, Catherine, and only you. If you stay in the cottage it will eventually possess you and be a danger to whoever stays with you. If and when you go from this place I really feel that you have a good chance of the force not following you, then in time, months even years, he will forget about you and he will return again to his own spirit world where he belongs."

I felt then as though nothing more terrible could happen to me. Amidyne had spoken in black and white. I had to move otherwise my family and my life could be in terrible danger, but I loved this cottage. I had been here many years now. I tried to think back far beyond to when the force had actually started. It was possibly even right here in the beginning when we had first moved in, but then it had lain quietly for many years undisturbed, until gradually it had grown to love me like his own dear wife.

The very thought sent my heart and senses reeling in turmoil. Only James, Adam, or Emma could help me at this awful time.

Adam frowned.

"It is really going to be hard for mum to move out. Are you positive that nothing can be done to get rid of this presence?"

His voice was strained as though coming from far away. She focused her blue eyes into his.

"There is nothing I or any other medium can do. It is a spirit of a different form. I can only advise you as to what can be done. It is far stronger than I spiritually, therefore it is a world beyond us a far superior one and one that we earth people really know little of. We can only take what is given and handed to us from that other world. We mediums have a gift but only a small gift that will take us into the secrets of the other world."

Her voice grew tired and her words began to trail off in a blur of exhaustion.

I stood up, cramped from sitting; Amidyne's silken shawl had slipped to the floor. I picked it up and folded it neatly on the chair beside her. I felt that we could ask no more of the clairvoyant that day. She had done well. It was now up to me to be strong and hold my family together as best I could.

Emma sat speechless as though she could not believe what she had heard. Adam sat moodily staring into space. I too sat as though in a spell, positively willing the phone to ring or for the dog to bark – anything at all that would break us all from this awful silence and dread of what lay ahead of us.

The clairvoyant at last slowly came out of her trance to glance worriedly at each one of our faces in turn. She then turned her eyes to mine.

"What will you do?" she asked as though she genuinely wanted to know.

I shook my head miserably then turned to Adam and Emma for support. They steadfastly kept their eyes firmly rooted to the ground. I was on my own for the time being anyway, shakily I turned to Amidyne.

"I can't really think at this point in time. It seems pointless staying here if there is not going to be an end to George, and really I have not the strength to take much more of it. To go – yes. I'll go away from here but the question is where to? If I move too far away I will not see my family. If I leave this house and go to live ten miles further up the road, George will no doubt find me. I just really do not know what to do, I just don't know the answer."

This was simply answered by another deathly silence, a window banged upstairs. Was it the wind getting up or was there someone up there. Nervously I looked towards the stairs. I was scared and for the moment had lost all meaning to life. I had lost my husband, my home and my future. What else would be next? Could it be me that George wanted me dead? For me to be in spirit along with him? Had he really forgotten his own dear wife? Could he possibly be waiting to push me down the cellar steps so that I too would die, so that he could take me to the second galaxy together with him? Was that really what he wanted?

I felt as though I wanted to shout out loudly at the top of my voice:

'NO you won't, you won't do it not to me.' The words formed and froze on my lips, though I could hear no sound coming from them. I made no sound. There was just the growing fear inside of me.

The front door flew noisily open – my thoughts pushed hastily aside – I jumped like a flash of lightning to my feet in fright.

"Hello folks, has anything exciting been happening."

James looked puzzled, taking in all of our dismal and gloomy expressions. This was the opening the clairvoyant had been waiting for; uneasily she looked at us each in turn.

"I do know how you all must be feeling." She looked uncertain for a moment then carried on.

"If I can possibly help in any way please do let me know at once. You have heard my advice to your mother that she must move far away from this place if she is ever to be happy and safe again. I just wish that I could banish the spirit away from your dwelling. Sadly, he is too strong even for me."

She hurriedly picked up her leather sequinned bag and looked uneasily towards the door as if a hundred hungry wolves were after her. Embarrassment – that was it – that was what she was. Embarrassed that she could not help us in dealing with this unknown force. It was as she said; it was far too forceful even for her great knowledge of the spirit kingdom. She wanted to help us but couldn't. All of a sudden I felt sorry for her; she was a professional and she could not help us any more in any way.

"I'll let you out."

James quietly opened the door letting in the warm sunshine that was blazing brightly in from outside.

My heart had risen when James had first entered the room. It now sank with a terrific crash back down to earth again. He would not be interested in what had been happening. He was going to leave me, leave me to sort out the mess in this now evil haunted cottage. I had gritted my teeth, I would show him. I would leave this place that had once been called home, leave it once and for all and start a completely new life far away from here.

Words, thought and meant with great bravado and strength, but only for a brief unrealistic few minutes. Thinking sensibly, where would I get the heart to do this without my husband by my side to give me hope and encouragement like he had always done in the past?

I heard the front door shut firmly with a bang, my husband was the only one to speak.

"Was she any good?" he enquired with a smile. The smile rapidly faded from his face on seeing our set and sour expressions.

"Has she told you anything different? Is it still with us? Is she able to make it go, get rid of it, send it away whatever to another plane, galaxy, spirit world?" His voice was getting higher by the second. He now was worried seriously worried like us, not only that but he also would be soon at breaking point like his family.

But with one big difference he would be leaving all of this behind him. We were not. Perhaps way ahead in the future yes, but how long would it take to sell a cottage – three months at the earliest – possibly one or even two years. The thought made me shudder and tremendously sick.

I tried; in fact I tried very hard to put a lightness into my voice that simply was not there. I then tried to relate as best as I could exactly what the clairvoyant had told us.

James sat, poker-faced, until I had finished. Clearly this had disturbed him as the corner of his mouth had started to twitch nervously.

"It sounds bad to me. What does everyone else think? Have you thought of a plan what to do? It does sound as though this force is getting more and more violent. I have only another three weeks before I move out, four at the most as I start my new position in Cornwall then, the sooner the better," James added grimly.

"You never told us you had got a new job in Cornwall." Adam spoke angrily. "After what you have just heard how on earth can you still leave mother here completely on her own? It's unsafe and you know it. Even if the cottage sells quickly she has got to find somewhere else to live, find a job, a home, get all packed up. It won't happen overnight. She is going to need a hell of a lot of support from all of us and that includes you as well. It's just not on to leave her like this. It's thoughtless and brutal of you and I am amazed that you can even contemplate going at all at the moment. You heard what mother said, she could seriously be in danger from this force."

Adam pushed his chair out of the way and stalked to the window, while Emma, without warning, burst into floods of tears.

James closed his eyes then stood up, picked up a cup of coffee and found the cup rattling on its saucer.

"Please yourself what you think!" he shouted then wandered through towards the settee and sat down, his hands clenched firmly round the cup. His hand still shaking slightly, he slowly took a deep breath trying hard to steady his breathing and his cup, then took a deep gulp of coffee and leaned back to close his eyes as though everything was just too much. I knew the feeling, I felt the same.

Behind him Emma was still sitting at the table. She sniffed then wiped the back of her hand across her eyes.

James drained his cup then swiftly got up and went towards the telephone.

"Where are you going?" I snapped.

"To phone."

"Phone where?" The answer was targeted straight back to me.

"The estate agents," James replied wearily. "I'm putting the cottage on the market this very instant, no ifs no buts, it's going up for sale now. I have simply had enough."

His hand tightened on the receiver and ignoring everyone he began to dial. He listened for several minutes then tried to dial again.

"What's wrong?" Adam asked sarcastically. "Are you incapable of dialling now?"

"I can't get a dialling tone." He shook the receiver and tried again. "It sounds as if there is a crossed line, as if someone is listening on the other end." I smiled.

"Perhaps somebody is," I said quietly, "it's happened before, it's up there you know listening to everything that is being said."

I could not believe that I had just said those words. It was as if someone had popped the words into my mouth, how very weird.

Emma, with a nervous glance, escaped thankfully into her father's study – his books piled high on the floor by his desk – it was as usual in a chaotic state. He would miss his little escape room when he moved out.

The room smelt strange, its usual comforting familiar smell had gone as though with it her father had gone too. Quietly she slipped out and back again to the dining room. All was not well in this house. There was something here. Even she could now feel its presence and it frightened her.

Nervously Emma headed towards her brother's side in the dining room.

"What's been happening?" she whispered.

"Dad's using the phone upstairs at this very moment and is instructing the sale of Broom Cottage to go ahead. It's awfully sad I know but it's got to be done. Mother has gone into the garden. She is very upset, she wants to move now as soon as possible. She's scared but the other part of her wants to stay. This cottage will be in her heart always, it's so sad."

They heard their father's footsteps coming down the stairs.

"Where is your mother?" he asked.

"She is upset and has gone into the garden with Holly." Adam spoke defensively.

"I do realise that neither you or Emma think well of me at this precise moment, but surely you must know that if it wasn't for this awful presence I would never have left your mother or this cottage. The truth is I just had to get away from it before I came to some harm, which I would have done and that is truth not fact. I travelled to Cornwall as I did not know where else to go. It had happy memories from the past for me and I thought I would be safe there, which of course I was."

He hesitated and looked decidedly uncomfortable.

"When I was staying in the hotel I got on friendly terms with a rather pleasant lady call Felicity. She lives on her own and we have been keeping in touch with each other. Last night we discussed living together for a while just to see how we get on. I have not told your mother yet of this. In fact, I don't really know how too, though I'll find some way of telling her over the next few days."

"How can you do this to her dad? Mum is going through hell at the moment. Everything is falling like a pack of cards around her, can't you wait a while, then tell her if you must when you have actually moved out."

"I know that she is going to need all the help that she can get." He twisted his hands nervously. "I have to tell her and soon. I really am sorry kids but surely I have to get far away from this presence here, otherwise it will kill me I know it will. I'll still be your father. You know that don't you? Perhaps one day when this shadow has gone we will get back together again."

"I doubt that very much."

Adam had spoken with hatred in his voice.

James' body shook with emotion he covered his hands over his face and wept. At last Adam touched his father's shoulder.

"Look we ought to talk later perhaps round my house." He lapsed into silence for a minute staring thoughtfully down at his feet.

"Let's leave it for a few days for things to get back to a little normality, if that is at all possible." His father's voice was muffled Adam, then suddenly grasped that he was deeply upset, more so than he had at first realised.

"That sounds a better idea to me. It will give us both time to calm down. In the meantime you're not going to let mother stay here on her own are you?"

He saw his father turn and face the window staring moodily ahead.

"You heard what I said on the phone. The cottage is already on the market. It's been on hold for months now, just awaiting our decision to go ahead."

"For heaven's sake all I'm asking is that you don't leave mother alone in this cottage at night, just answer yes or no that's all I'm asking." Adam raised his voice, his face flushed with sudden anger.

"I won't leave her for several weeks yet as I told you, though I cannot be her keeper. I will be with her at night for the time being. During the days I cannot make such definite agreements. We are both two adults with different friends and commitments which means she will possibly be alone at odd times until such a time that I leave for Cornwall. After that time you will all have to work it out for yourselves. I cannot be responsible for anything more."

With that James went out slamming the door behind him.

Bleakly James and Emma glanced at each other wondering what to do next. A movement behind them made them each jump nervously.

Their mother was looking at them, looking pale and tired, and suddenly much older than her years.

"Both of you go home now, my dears, I will be alright, I promise."

"Oh mum," whispered Emma. "You look so tired would you like to come home with me and stay a few nights?"

"No, your father will be here and I have plans to make. Come again tomorrow evening if you want. We will be able to talk things through more rationally then. Go on off you go, good night."

They shut the door quietly behind them.

I had not really wanted them to go. I already felt so much alone, restless and lost. Perhaps a little light supper would help; read a little; listen to some lively music; have a hot bath and go to bed early.

236

James that night told me of Felicity. It had not come as a total shock. I had felt deep down that he would find somebody else and now he had.

I had too much pride to rant and rave like some women would have done; I was hurt, sad, tearful and afraid of the future. Deeply afraid, I trembled at the thought of being on my own. I shrank from it and dreaded every day and tomorrow ahead of me without James. He had been my bridge and my shoulder to lean on for many years and it had been a solid one up until now, and to think it was all for a spirit by the name of George.

Tearful once again, I resolutely turned towards bed and sleep. That was the only thing that would wipe out all this unhappiness for a while at least. When I wake in the morning, I must look towards the future and not look back. I had plans to make and quickly if I were to move and move I must and soon.

Time has passed slowly. It was now four weeks later and James had only just recently moved out. He had gone silently without making any fuss. He had done the cowardly thing and left a brief note to say only a few things – like he would always love me, he would be in touch, and to take care.

What a simple cold note. He had not even left a contact address. What did I care anyway, though if the truth, be known there were lots.

I vowed in that moment to make my life even busier and made plans for the future now that my husband had gone. Adam and Emma were to take turns in sleeping the night at Broome Cottage with me so that I would not be alone.

Those first few weeks after James had gone were quite pleasant ones, much to my surprise, and my children were good company which took the edge off a little so that I did not miss my husband quite do much as I thought I would have done. Gradually I got more and more used to him not being there.

It had all been such a rush up until now, the packing, the storing of furniture, and trying to arrange my new life, separating or trying to separate myself from James. I had little time to think and welcomed the exhaustion every evening; it meant that I did not dwell on things so much.

I had given up my Accounts job. I desperately needed time to find a new domain for myself in a new county. I had chosen Essex, where my roots had been many years ago, where I had been born.

I had been fortunate enough to find a very small cottage on the wild northeastern coast of Essex. The cottage was old, quaint and cosy, with strangers for neighbours for a little while anyway, until I got to know them. Downstairs there was only the one living room with a small kitchen and an even smaller bathroom next to it. Upstairs there were two bedrooms almost identical in size.

These had a sloping floor with a low-beamed ceiling. I simply loved it, but would I have the strength and determination to do it, to move here and leave my beloved Broome Cottage for good? It would take some doing.

Even though James had already gone, the last seven weeks had passed by more quickly. I had missed him tremendously. He had been part of my life for the last twenty-five years. That was a long time. I had missed him but Adam and Emma had helped a lot by staying with me and we had taken turns in shedding our tears.

I had felt so much stronger this last week. The force appeared to have gone which made me feel so much more relaxed and happier, and now I only had the major problem of staying or selling. In a way it was exciting. I had a buyer ready and waiting and now it looked as though I had found the ideal cottage just waiting for an offer. I had travelled down to Essex that morning especially to look round it again. To me it was perfect.

When I got home I would have to make up my mind and decide. In the meantime I had a long journey home. It would be dark by the time I reached Broome Cottage. I had been silly not to ring Emma to tell her that I would be home that night after all. I had got used to having someone always there in the next room.

Glancing at my watch, which said eight-thirty, my brain quickly calculating the time that I would take to reach there. It would be nearly midnight; I could not expect either of them to wait up that long. They each had work the next day. I made up my mind. I must brave it alone there tonight or else stay in a bed and breakfast overnight. I unwisely chose Broome Cottage.

The drive from Essex proved a long slow one. Night driving had never been one of my good points, nor would it ever prove to be.

Eventually, I sleepily drove into the driveway. The cottage was in darkness. My heart sank. I did not really want to go in. Would it be too late to drive round to Adam's? I decided that it was. I had a torch somewhere in the car. Where was it? At last after much fumbling I discovered it.

Feeling much better having located the torch, I swung the main beam onto the front door and felt for my keys. It was very quiet not even a rustle in the trees beyond. Hastily I walked to the front door. How I wished that I had asked Adam or Emma to leave a light on.

The door felt stiff to open as though already it knew that I was going to leave. With a final hard shove it opened. Immediately I smelt the heavenly scent of roses upon entering Broome Cottage; it was gorgeous whatever was it. Once however past the entrance hall it seemed to have disappeared for a moment. Puzzled, I looked round, no flowers on the table. Where had it come from I wondered?

I dropped my handbag onto the kitchen table. Time for coffee I thought, then bed. It was late and I was extremely tired after my long drive. Holly was pleased to be home. At least I had her for company.

I quickly made my drink, and was about to turn the radio on for company when I heard a sound which seemed to come from the hall. It sounded like a faint husky laugh. Nervously I tiptoed across the floor. I opened the door a crack and peered out into the hall.

It was dark out there, but I could see a thin line of light showing from the dining room. Opening the door further, I peered up the stairs. Everything there was dark and silent. I looked towards the dining room again – still the faint light showed beneath the door. The next door to it was the cellar door which stood wide open.

Who had left it open? Had Emma been down there and forgotten to shut it?

Calling Holly to my side, I strode purposely to turn the dining room light off and to shut the cellar door.

As my hand went to touch the switch I saw a woman standing in the corner of the room. In the fraction of a second that she was there, I saw her grey hair, her long blue gown and I knew that somewhere I had seen this person before and then she was gone, leaving only the scent of a flowery rosy perfume behind – the same scent that had been there when I had first opened the front door that evening.

I backed towards the open cellar my eyes still on the spot where the woman had stood. I was conscious of the black rough stormy night outside. Had it created this vision inside my head? Was it imagination or had I really seen it?

Suddenly, as if from nowhere, I felt an almighty push in the middle of my back. I staggered and frantically tried to hold on to the open cellar door, I felt another stronger firmer push which seemed to knock every breath from my body. I faintly heard Holly growling beside me, then felt someone's warm breath on my cheek. Something or somebody was trying to push me down into the cellar. I saw the steep concrete steps before me and the darkness below. I felt the warm sweet horrible breath on my neck this time. I must move and move quickly. With all my strength I slammed the cellar door shut and turned the key. Then took the stairs two at a time and ran into my bedroom slamming the door as hard as I could behind me, realising in my frenzy that Holly was on the other side of the door. I couldn't let her in, my hands and body were now frozen solid and paralysed with fear.

I tried to think rationally and not panic. It was no use putting the chair up against the door; spirits could walk through them couldn't they? Nevertheless I felt myself dragging the dressing table up against it, somehow it made me feel better if not safer.

Shakily I sat myself on the bed, desperately trying to clear my head so that I could think. Who had pushed me? Why does George want me dead, but it was a woman that I had seen. Wasn't it? Who was it? I had seen that face before but where, oh please let me remember. Surely it was not George wanting me dead. He loved me so much, so then who was it?

The scent of flowery perfume came once again creeping under the door, through every crack and crevice, or was she now here in this bedroom with me, was it a she?

Suddenly, as though a flashlight had burst inside my head, I knew without a shadow of doubt who the scented perfume belonged to. It was, it must of course be Alice who was George's wife. She had died a few months earlier, I remembered the clairvoyant telling me. She had come to live and be with her husband George. He would not go to her on the second galaxy so she in her spirit world had decided to come and be here with him in this cottage where once they had been so very happy.

I felt at once an intense fear all around me. She wanted me out of the way. She wanted me dead so that she could have the cottage to herself with her husband. I was a threat to her. She knew that George already loved me, and she did not want that, she wanted her husband to herself without me.

I could hear Holly whining outside the bedroom door, wanting and willing me to let her in. What on earth was I to do? My eyes suddenly blurred with tears. I tried hard to think. Could I climb out of the window to escape to the car? But my keys lay on the table downstairs in the kitchen. I heard Holy whining more frantically this time. Somehow I must summon up all my courage to let Holly in, then make a dash for it no matter what, down the stairs and out into the car.

For a moment, just for a few brief seconds, I closed my eyes. The phone on the landing just outside my bedroom door started to ring unexpectedly.

Who on earth could it be at this time of night? Was it a trick to get me out of the room or was it Adam or Emma checking that I was at home and safe?

Without a second thought I pushed the dressing table out of the way and rushed out onto the landing, half sobbing I grabbed the phone to my ear.

"Mother it's me Adam, are you ok?"

I took a deep breath. "You must come over at once, right now."

My voice sounded hysterical I knew that.

"Did you hear me, I'll be in the bedroom I'm so afraid, be quick."

I heard an exclamation of impatience, then my son's voice saying, "I'm on my way keep calm."

With that I slammed the receiver down and fled back to my bedroom.

I lay on the bed not daring to move a muscle, hearing my rasping pounding chest, listening for every new sound, my eyes darting quickly here and there around the room looking for what? That I did not know, possibly for the gowned figure that I seen earlier downstairs.

I knew that I was utterly alone in this house – no one at all to help me. I glanced over my shoulder and shivered. I had a headache which was growing stronger by the second. A draught seemed to suddenly appear in the room – an icy draught that had not been there before. I looked again behind me, a faint haze was forming, then a shadow hovered around me bringing with it an even more intense cold.

I shut my eyes firmly to blot out the vision but only for a second. Swiftly I opened them again to see that the shadow was standing directly in front of me. It was in the figure of a man, a bent old man. Was it George this time? Was he here to protect me? Was that possible?

My first instinct was to run, to get out, down the stairs until Adam came. Was it one spirit up here or two? George and his wife Alice?

I had gone past all sense of reasoning. I had to get out and now. I gently opened the bedroom door and turned towards the stairs.

My body stiffened as the scent of flowers wafted up the stairs to greet me, stronger this time much stronger than before. Paralysed with fear, my brain numbly registered the fact that both George and his wife must be here now in this very cottage. Was it really possible and who would believe me?

Clinging to the banisters I made my way slowly down the steep staircase; it was as I put my foot on the last bottom step that I first saw the movement ahead. I stiffened then froze like a statue of ice.

"Is there anyone there?" My voice echoed and sounded thin and frightened in the silence.

There was no answer. Silence.

"Who is it?" I called again timidly.

I was answered by the rattle of rain on the windows as yet another squall of wind hit the cottage. I sniffed hard. The scent of flowery perfume had completely disappeared. It was when I pushed back the curtains and stared out at the blackness beyond, I could still see the rain teeming down the pane of glass. I felt empty, alone, and utterly desolate.

"Please Adam," I prayed. "Come quickly before it is too late."

It was scarcely two minutes later that I saw the headlights of Adam's car chasing through the trees.

A huge sigh of relief escaped from her mouth. "Thank God," I breathed and raced to the front door to let him in.

As I opened it an icy blast of air rushed in. I knew that I was screaming. I could even hear myself and it was terrifying.

"I'm here Adam, hurry up," frantically trying to hold the door open as I spoke. It was as if someone was trying to force it to close. I could see Adam running to the door, straining against the force of the wind. I pushed the door open wider, and felt the perspiration pouring down my face in the effort to keep it open. Unknown hands were trying to keep Adam out.

As my son entered the cottage I saw his eyes taking in the dim light of the lamp, casting a soft glow over the room.

"I'm so sorry Adam I should not have come here tonight, not on my own. George is here the, spirit of George I mean and," numbly I paused for a minute struggling hard to keep the tears at bay, "I think a second spirit is here in this cottage with him."

Heart rending sobs now escaped from my lips.

"The second spirit I'm sure is of George's wife. She tried to push me down the cellar steps, she wants me dead," I whispered, "wants me out of the way so that she can take George back to the second galaxy where she and he belongs."

Adam's face turned white.

"It's unbelievable what you're saying. In other words it looks as though George wants you to stay, is that it?"

I nodded miserably.

"I don't think I can bear it a moment longer here," I whispered.

At that precise moment the rose scented perfume wafted slowly in again through the door filling the entire room with its nauseating scent.

Grabbing hard at Adam's sleeve, "Can you smell it too, tell me you can smell it?" Grimly he nodded.

"Yes I can, does that belong to the spirit of Alice?"

I whispered. "I think so," then looked fearfully at the door.

"Take me away Adam now; we are in such terrible danger if we stay here much longer."

"Is that your case?" He pointed swiftly to the corner where I had dropped it only such a short while, earlier.

"Is there anything else that you're needing before we go?"

"No only Holly."

"Where is she?" my son quietly asked.

Shakily I looked for her at my side, the room was empty. "Holly, Holly come here!" I could hear myself shouting her name over and over again, but no Holly came, no answering bark not even a whine.

Weeping hysterically at my son's side I spoke almost in a whisper.

"Perhaps she got in my bedroom and I shut the door on her without me realising it."

Grabbing my hand, Adam looked at me with real fear in his eyes.

"We must keep together and make a run for it, but first we must look for Holly. We cannot possibly leave her here without us. We must head up the stairs first to your bedroom."

Placing a foot on the bottom step, he paused and looked up, his hand firmly on the worn banister rail. It was cold upstairs. Even from here on the ground floor where it was pleasantly warm he could feel the light touch of a draught on his face. As he climbed he realised that he was praying. We reached my bedroom door, both bursting the door open.

"Holly are you there, Holly come on." I could hear Adam calling her name over and over again but all was silent.

He shivered, his mother was right it was very cold up here, strangely cold. It had an odd atmosphere too.

Adam stopped in his tracks trying to resist the urge to turn round and look over his shoulder.

He was imagining it of course. It was his mother that had told him the room was haunted, hadn't she?

"Holly!" Adam shouted again but the room was completely empty, no dog, no Holly. Where was she? There was no sound at all, no whimpering or barking as though she had never been.

The sound of the wind had dropped all of a sudden, as though it had been blanketed out by fog or mist. Everywhere was silent – not a whisper anyway at all.

"She was up here!" I screamed. "Only a short while ago she was whining for me to let her in, but I was too frightened to unlock the door, and then I opened it to answer the phone to you."

A look of horror was written all over my son's face.

Brokenly I drew breath. Where was she?

"I didn't hear or see Holly after that."

"Adam sighed. He wasn't sure what he was expecting to happen. An apparition perhaps, whatever it was not going to be pleasant.

"Hold on to me don't let go whatever happens, grab my trousers anything just don't let go. We must search everywhere room by room. This top landing first. Come on there's no time to waste."

I did as I was told, too miserable and numb to speak. Where was my dog, my faithful loving friend for so long?

Slowly we opened each door to look inside. All were empty. The scented perfume followed us. It was still there though it seemed even more powerful than ever before.

"Come on downstairs as fast as you can," his hand still gripping mine like a vice.

"Where can she be, what has happened to her. I'm so afraid Adam, supposing we don't find her?"

My feeble mutterings were being blown to the wind; already Adam had pulled me down the stairs and reached the hall below.

"Holly," I heard my voice calling out feebly but still no answering bark.

"The dining room, first." Adam spoke desperately, "then the kitchen and beyond that the cellar."

A door banged noisily behind us making us both jump. There must be a door open somewhere. Anxiously I looked round, the presence of the perfume had gone, but in the distance I could hear the wind picking up again, followed by a distinct chill in the air.

Vaguely I could hear Adam speaking. He was pointing to the kitchen door. "Did you shut it earlier? It's usually kept open isn't it?" he asked questioning me.

Worriedly I turned to look towards the kitchen door.

"I never ever shut that door, perhaps that was the one that we heard shut when we were on the stairs," I whispered back.

He frowned. "I don't like this at all. There is something really sinister in this cottage. It's eerie and it's haunted."

I could see the terrified fear in his face. What was hiding in the kitchen? What would we find? There was only one way in which to find out.

We did not see the figure behind us, the woman in the long dress and the dark cloak, the woman with madness and hatred in her eyes.

Adam hesitated for one brief moment. "Keep with me," then he strode purposely towards the kitchen door.

Silently I followed, the cold air drawing in like an icy claw around us.

Adam's hand closed stealthily round the oak handle of the door, opening it slowly, quietly inch by inch until at last it stood wide open and we could see within.

No sound at all escaped from the kitchen, it was empty.

I felt faint, weak and very much afraid. What were we going to find in this cottage that I had once so loved, and which I now hated.

No sign of Holly rushing out to greet us, my son's voice sounded frightened and tetchy. "Where on earth is she? A dog just can't disappear into thin air! We must try the cellar next; we can't possibly go without her. Come on we must be quick."

It was as we stood by the huge kitchen table that we both heard a soft whimper. The atmosphere was beginning to clear slightly; we both stood rooted to the spot. Outside the window a car rattled past the driveway, then all fell silent once more.

Carefully we strained our ears for more sounds.

"Did you hear that whimper?"

I nodded.

"I think it came from near the bay window over there." Adam whispered.

He pointed to the furthest corner from us; again we both felt the presence, as though it had taken the place of the awful scented perfume that had clung to us earlier.

Could this possibly be George that was now with us? Were we now safer with him? Could it be Alice who had the power and hatred to push me down the cellar steps; she who was the evil mad one who was now trying to destroy me to get her husband back to the spirit world.

A horrendous thought entered my head. If she had the mystic powers to do that, to physically harm me, what else could she do to my dog? I shuddered violently. "Where would this nightmare end?"

I felt Adam tugging at my arm.

"There it is again I'm sure it's Holly whimpering." He literally dragged me across the room.

There in the corner folded into the shadows lay my dog. With tears pouring down my face, I ran over to her side, dropping my body to the floor in my haste to reach her.

Holly was shivering pathetically with cold, fright and fear – possibly a mixture of them all. She was crouching as though she was utterly petrified. Feebly she struggled to get up but couldn't, as though she was too weak. All the strength and energy from her body seemed to have been taken out of her.

She whined again and tried to wag her tail but failed dismally. Adam gathered her up in one powerful sweep of his arms.

Every nerve of his body was taut and strained. His voice echoed the same thoughts as my own.

"Mother we have to get out of here fast. I'll carry the dog; you grab the case and leave everything else until daylight. Did you hear that? Just let's get the hell out of here while we are still alive."

Struggling with my tears, I could only nod.

He was speaking again.

"Say goodbye to the cottage mum as we go out. You must leave this place and never ever return again. Do you hear what I'm saying to you? This is the finish, now run let's just get out of here.

I never ever returned to that cottage again.

I am now writing this six months later. It had been a heartbreaking way to leave my cottage after that terrifying last night. I used to have nightmares about it but they are getting few and far between now.

I had stayed with Emma after that. I had no wish to visit or to live there again. It was full of unhappy, hateful, sad and terrifying moments, which I hoped never ever to experience again.

James had been asked to come down at weekends to help Adam pack and empty the cottage and store some of the furniture for when I moved. It had taken them some considerable time and they only visited it in daylight.

They told me it was now all at peace. George must have returned to the world of spirit, probably with his wife, contented that they were now together where they belonged.

Afterwards when the clairvoyant had heard our story about that last terrifying night, she said that the spirit or force could possibly return again next month, next year who knows? I guess that I will never ever be certain of that, only that they could return at any time to Broome Cottage.

It was far too big a risk for me to take.

I bought the little cottage on the North Essex coast not too far from where I had lived whilst still a child – the cottage that I had viewed on the day of that last evil night at Broome Cottage.

I'm away from my family, which I miss sometimes, but I am away from other sources and spirits. There is nothing now to haunt me and I am at peace.

Holly is now recovered after her traumatic experience and is resting quietly beside me as I end this story. She is happy as she runs in the River Blackwater instead of the forest.

Who knows if the force will return or not? That I will never know for sure.